# THE BLOOD BEAST MUTATIONS

CARL JOHN LEE

This book is a work of fiction.
No part of this publication may be reproduced or transmitted in any form without written permission from the author.

Cover art by Jason Laser

Copyright © 2020 Carl John Lee
All rights reserved.
ISBN:9798645838263

*For HJK*
*You know why*

# PART I

Darkest Before The Dawn

# 1

Like a half-remembered dream, my old life no longer seems real.

No one's does, I guess.

We should have listened, should have moved faster. But then, no one saw it coming. Not like *this*, anyway.

At first, it was surreal, a fantasy. We laughed about it, made jokes, safe in the knowledge that it couldn't possibly happen to us.

They said it came from China, and the president stood there and told us it was fake news, and that soon the cases would be down to zero. *Don't worry,* he said, *we have the best predictions, the best doctors, the best words.*

But all he really had were the best excuses.

The best bullshit.

Now it's July, a boiling New York summer, and we're afraid to leave the apartment. This time last year, I'd been sitting in the park with my wife, ninety degrees in the shade. She had stripped to her underwear, lying face down and enjoying the sun, her bra unclasped. She was twenty-five, beautiful, with auburn hair that danced around her shoulders, and man, did she look incredible just lounging there in her little red panties.

Life had been so good back then. I remember we got home after dinner and made love all evening, until we fell asleep in each other's arms, naked and content.

It seems so long ago, and I suppose it is.

The world is fucked, and it's not even our fault.

Makes a change, huh?

# 2

Twelfth of July was when it all went to hell in a handbasket, as my mom used to say, before the virus took her. In the days leading up to it, we had seen the videos on social media, and dismissed them.

You can't blame us.

It was crazy...unbelievable.

My wife — sorry, I mean Cassie, she hates when I call her *my wife,* says it makes her think of Borat — had woken me early. She sat on the bed in a baggy tee and a pair of my shorts, shaking me til I reluctantly wiped the sleep from my eyes.

I was all out of whack with the lockdown. That's what happens when you've got no reason to get up, no reason to go to bed. Your internal clock goes haywire. Cassie insisted on always rising at eight, and getting dressed. Said it helped create a sense of routine. Me, I preferred to lie in. What did it matter if I got up at eight, or ten, or five-fuckin'-thirty? I had no job to go to. The bar I worked in closed permanently round about the time of the second spike in cases, after

President Dipshit had ordered the reopening of the economy. That second lockdown was the last straw for most small businesses. With no income, and no government relief, they had no choice but to shut down permanently.

"Take a look at this," said Cassie, handing me her phone. I was half-asleep, but the sun blasted into the bedroom, burning my eyes like a vampire awoken from a centuries-long slumber, with the attitude to match.

"What fuckin' time is it?"

"Seven," she said. Already I could hear the protestors marching through the streets, chanting their goddam slogans through megaphones.

*"End the lockdown."*

*"Freedom is a right."*

The usual BS.

I wanted to head down there, grab that fucking loudspeaker, and shove it so far up someone's ass that their farts would echo for ten blocks.

But that would be a bad idea. They were armed, the lot of them, pistols and assault rifles and bullet proof vests three sizes too small. They wore jungle camouflage pants and desert camouflage jackets, like they figured if they took a left on Fifth Avenue they'd end up in the Sahara Desert. These men — and women — were dangerous, and not just because of their weapons, or their beliefs.

They were dangerous because of their stupidity.

"Dan, come on, you gotta see this," she said, snapping me out of my drowsy morning thoughts, and there was something in her voice that made me sit up and pay attention.

I took the phone from her. There was a video already playing. I reached for my glasses and tried to put them on one-handed, jabbing myself in the eye.

"Jesus," I said. "It's too early for cat videos."

"Just watch. Please."

And so I did. At first I wasn't sure what I was looking at. A brief shot of a red smear on a shower curtain, and then the video ended. I looked at Cassie, too tired to shrug.

"What was that?"

She snatched the phone back, and tapped at the screen. "Watch from the start," she said, sighing in that theatrical way I found so endearing.

It was clearer now. The interior of a hospital. I had gotten so used to seeing the insides of hospitals on the news that I sometimes felt I lived in one. The camera panned along rows of beds, the white curtains drawn in front of most, and I absently wondered what the death toll would be today. Would this be the day it topped four-hundred-thousand?

"Dan, pay attention," said Cassie.

Someone on the video was speaking.

*"This is the scene inside the emergency ward at"* — there was a beep as the name of the hospital was cut out — *"Memorial. Something's happening...the virus seems to be mutating."*

"Oh shit, what now?" I said, unable to muster much enthusiasm for this latest development. People were already dying in their thousands, no, *millions* across the globe, and the so-called murder hornets had recently arrived in the States, while armed lunatics roamed the streets out of a desperate need to feel in control of something. A mutation in the virus was just another slap in the face. They didn't even have a vaccine yet, and it was mutating.

We were truly fucked.

"You woke me up for this?" I said.

"Just wait." She sounded pissed-off, so I decided to shut

up and watch like she asked, or I'd never convince her to join me under the covers afterwards.

*"It started last night, or at least that's when we noticed it,"* said the man in the video. He had a British accent. *"Something was wrong...wrong with their insides..."*

He walked through the hospital, the camera — I suppose it was his phone — shaking with each step. It made me dizzy, like that time Cassie had forced me to watch *The Blair Witch Project*. There were dozens of beds, the occupants hooked up to ventilators, some sleeping, some doubled up in agony, choking and screaming, reaching their hands out towards the doctor.

Doctor?

I wasn't sure. A medical professional of some capacity, I wagered. Or a patient, or a visitor, or an undercover journalist. His hand came into shot, grabbing the curtain and pulling it aside.

"What the hell is that?" I said, not realizing I was speaking out loud.

There was something on the bed — some*one*, I suppose, though I didn't see how it could be...real. I squinted at the screen, at the flat, lifeless human-shaped piece of skin. It was hard to tell where the person ended and the blood began. It soaked the white sheets, and I could hear it dripping onto the floor.

There was an almighty roar from offscreen.

When I think about it now, it sends shivers down my spine.

The camera spun, and there it was, hurtling towards the cameraman at full-pelt. It was onscreen for a fraction of a second, before the camera fell to the floor, staring lifelessly up at the curtain. A spray of blood hit the stiff fabric, running down the folds in smooth red lines.

"Pretty intense," I said, handing the phone back to Cassie. I could tell by her face she thought it was real, and it made me laugh. When she gets concerned, this serious look comes over her, like she's performing an operation or taking an exam. "Hey," I said, holding her hand. "It's not real."

"I know," she smiled, but I wasn't convinced. When you've lived with someone for a few years, you learn to read them like a book. All their quirks, their eccentricities...you get used to them, you know what to look for.

The important thing is that you learn to love them.

So when Cassie pulled her concerned face, I cracked up. Looking back, I was an asshole. But come on, I've said it already, and I'll say it again and again until I'm blue in the face — no one took it seriously. More videos emerged from hospitals across the country, each rejected as elaborate hoaxes. After the third, most people stopped paying attention.

It was the Harlem Shake of 2020.

We had bigger things to worry about, like the global pandemic, and the maniac in charge, and the armed patrols, and the fucking murder hornets. Did I mention the murder hornets?

Man, talk about bad timing.

I took Cassie's phone from her, and she tried to get it back, and I ended up tickling her, and whad'ya know, soon I had her shorts off (my shorts, technically, but they looked good on her). I was already naked — I told you, it was one hot summer — and then we were making love again, though it didn't feel like love. It felt primal, desperate, like we were trying to fuck away the horror that surrounded us. In moments of darkness, you have to look for the light wherever you can find it.

*It's always darkest just before dawn,* Cassie liked to say.

But what do you do if dawn never comes?

# 3

CASSIE FELL SICK AROUND THE FOURTH OF JULY.

At first we thought it was a result of the party, and by party, I mean getting together with some friends over Zoom. Everyone was there — Jim and Beth, who lived on the other side of the city, Carol and Lucy from Arkansas, even Pat and Ahmed, joining us live from the UK. It's funny how we spent years worrying about technology pushing people apart, but then it became the only thing keeping us together.

Pat and Ahmed were subdued. I figured it was due to the time difference, not realizing what was going on over there. We knew it was grim — their Prime Minister was almost as bad as the clown in charge of the States — but had no idea *how* grim. I guess the mutations hit them first, though back then it was all conjecture, the ravings of YouTube conspiracy theorists and quacks.

We got drunk, real drunk, and Cassie produced a pack of Rothmans. Neither of us had smoked in, what, three years? It's hard to say. Time moves differently now. Anyway, We had a couple each, and it tasted good, reminded us of what things were like before, when you could smoke in clubs and bars. Not that we missed the smell, mind you.

We missed the freedom.

We hit bed about four, so drunk that even sex was off the menu, and I swear we could have slept for a week, if Cassie hadn't woken with a coughing fit. I figured it was the cigarettes, you see. That's the problem. You never think it's gonna happen to you. Her cough got worse, and I left the apartment to go to the drugstore. I had read somewhere not to use cough medicine, as it helped the virus, but I didn't know what to believe.

Don't use Ibuprofen...*do* use Ibuprofen...don't cover your face...*do* cover your face...

Every time I looked online, there was new, conflicting information. It got so bad we decided not to google things anymore.

When I came back, Cassie was hugging the toilet bowl, legs curled up beneath her.

"I've been sick," she said, her voice quivering. I made my way over, put my hand on her shoulder, and through her thin cotton tee I could feel the clammy heat radiating from her skin. The inside of the bowl was splashed red with blood, so bright against the porcelain, almost fake, like in a movie from the seventies. Cassie looked up at me with wide, tearful eyes, then coughed again. The blood splattered my shirt and the crotch of my pants.

"Oh god, I'm sorry," she cried, which only made her cough again.

"Don't worry about it," I said, kneeling beside her, holding her hair back as she ejected another lungful of blood into the bowl.

When she was finished, she quietly said, "I don't want you to get it too."

*The Blood Beast Mutations*

---

I called an ambulance, and the lady on the end of the line said one would be with us in the next twenty-four hours. I wanted to scream down the phone at her, tell her how sick Cassie was, but what good would screaming do? We were all in the same boat.

At around ten that evening, I saw the paramedics coming along the street. There was another group of protestors, and they shouted at the medics, hurling their signs and spitting on them. One asshole in a fucking cowboy hat lunged at them, threatening to rip their face-masks off.

I wept openly, wondering what had happened to society, to empathy. The buzzer sounded a few minutes later, and I let them in. The rest is a blur. All I remember is them taking her away, and a medic telling me they couldn't test me yet, they had run out, but they would send me one through the mail when they became available.

I didn't care about me, though. Only Cassie. We said our goodbyes, and as she was led out the door, she told me she loved me. The way she said it sounded like it was the last time she ever would, and it broke my heart.

---

I watched them leave from our seventh-storey window. The protestors had moved on, the ambulance able to pull up outside. They loaded her into the back, and the vehicle pulled away. The TV was on in the background, *The Naked Gun* playing. I sat and watched it for a while in a daze, then fell asleep on the couch around two in the morning.

All I wanted was for Cassie to be with me.

## 4

THE PRESIDENT — I SAY THAT, BUT HE'S NOT MY PRESIDENT, never will be — stood in a room of lackeys, unmasked, delivering one of those rambling, incoherent speeches. Apparently, five-hundred-thousand deaths would be an excellent result. He had said the same about four-hundred-thousand, and three, and two.

"Just keep moving those goalposts, motherfucker," I said to the screen. I was drunk. It had been a week since Cassie had been admitted to hospital, and three days since I heard anything. The phone-lines, when I tried to call, were always busy. I sent emails, DMs on social media, but no one ever replied.

In my darkest moments, when I drank one Scotch too many, I wondered if she was dead. Part of me dreaded the phone ringing, in case I wasn't prepared for the news.

That was the eleventh of July, the day before everything turned to shit.

One journalists asked the president about the rumors of some mutation to the virus. We had all seen the videos by now, from Europe and Asia. Half-glimpsed horrors, never clear enough to conclusively call real or fake. Well, the president had made *his* mind up.

"*That's a disgusting question, you know, really disgusting… you should be ashamed,*" he said. "*That's the lamestream media for you, folks…we have, and I want to make this very clear…there is no mutation, not a mutation like you understand…it's clear to me that, and I know a lot about mutations, more than anyone in this room, maybe the country…and we have some brilliant scientists, the best. Your numbers are down, low ratings, so you try—*"

I switched it off, wanting to put my foot through the screen, but then what else could I do if not watch TV? Sirens wailed past. I had never heard so many, and do I need to remind you, I live in fucking *New York*. For a city supposedly on lockdown, there was a lot of police activity. Maybe the gangs had decided to unite, to overthrow the governor or something. I poured myself another drink and shivered in the heat. Was I coming down with it too? It had been seven days…surely I would have developed symptoms by now? Cassie and I, we shared a small apartment, we slept in the same bed, used the same dishes, kissed each other…no way I didn't have it, unless I was asymptomatic. But when I thought of that, I had to consider the fact that I may have infected Cassie, so instead I chose to drink.

I looked out the window. More and more protestors, their ranks swelling every day. Some of the new recruits were normal people. No guns, no camo, just everyday folks looking for something to occupy their time, something to believe in, a reason to exist other than heading to the grocery store once a week. New York apartments are not made with home cooking in mind, I'll tell you that for a fact.

One guy — older-looking, snow-white hair — carried a placard that read, HAPPY TO DIE FOR THE ECONOMY

I smiled ruefully. I bet that same guy could routinely be

found harassing women on their way to abortion clinics. Some people are only pro-life when you're a fetus. After that, all bets are off, *unleash the hounds!*

LIVE FREE OR DYE, said other sign, this one carried by a middle-aged woman in a tie-dye vest. I doubted it was a fiendishly clever, ironic point she was making.

It would be foolish to leave for the grocery store while these fuckers were out there — anyone wearing a mask and observing social distancing was an immediate target — so I waited until they had passed, flipping mindlessly through a paperback. After a while I realized I'd read the same page ten, fifteen times. The crowd had moved on, and the streets were silent again, apart from the distant, haunting wail of sirens.

I grabbed my phone, but not my wallet — no one accepted cash anymore — and left my apartment for the first time in days. The complex was eerily quiet, and I took the elevator down. Walking the streets felt like a strange and confusing dream. They were nearly empty. I passed two people on three-block journey to the store, both of them avoiding me by stepping onto the deserted road. I nodded as they did so, and they nodded back. Nodding was the new smiling, for what's the point in smiling if no one can see your face? Cassie used to watch that dumb show, *America's Next Top Model*, and the presenter would go on about 'smising', the art of smiling with your eyes.

Fuck that.

I would continue to nod, until there was no one left to nod at.

---

The OPEN sign flashed in the window, and I entered,

browsing the near-empty aisles. The second lockdown had sparked another panicked stockpiling of goods, but it was mainly the big stores that had been hit. I picked up a couple of tv dinners, some toilet paper, fruit and veg, the usual. I grabbed a candy bar, Cassie's favorite, and put it in my cart.

"For when she's home," I said to myself. Like a lost child, I started to cry in the middle of the store. I knew I shouldn't be out — I should isolate myself for another week — but I had to shop, and nowhere was offering deliveries til at least August. What the fuck was I supposed to do, eat my own leg?

"Hey Dan," said Larry from behind the checkout, a plastic screen separating us. "How's tricks?"

"Up and down," I said. One of the worst things about the pandemic was the small talk. You couldn't talk about the Knicks anymore, or the Yankees, or any sport. Nothing was happening, except the crushingly slow annihilation of mankind. "How bout you? Business still slow?"

Larry grunted behind his mask, his gloved hands scanning my goods. "Nah, I'm beating them off with a stick," he said, and laughed mirthlessly. "How's Cass? Not seen her for a long time."

"She's..."

I couldn't tell him she was sick. He'd think I had the virus, and if I did, why was I out?

"She's fine. Painting a lot. She's real good, Larry. One day I think she'll exhibit them in a gallery or something."

Larry nodded. "Yeah, one day. For sure. When all this is..." He seemed to run out of steam, or perhaps he had used his quota of positivity for the day.

"When all this is over," I said, finishing his thought.

"Yeah. My wife says it can't rain all the time."

I thought that was actually the little girl in *The Crow*, but didn't mention it.

"Here's hoping, Larry." I packed up my bags and headed for the door.

"Be careful out there, Dan."

I turned to look at him. "The protestors? They won't be back for a while."

"I don't mean those sons-a-bitches. I mean…"

"What? That bullshit on the internet? Larry, come on…"

"That's what we said a few months ago," he said. "Now look at us."

"That's different," I said, not sure who I was trying to convince. "A virus is one thing. But…this? Sorry, Larry, I don't believe in—"

"Monsters? Neither do I. But there's a lot of stuff out there, Dan. Every day there're more and more of those videos. My kids show 'em to me. I'll be honest, Dan. I'm scared. I'm scared shitless."

"Me too," I said, and it was the truth.

## 5

I GOT THE CALL AT SEVEN THE NEXT MORNING.

It woke me from a fraught and drunken sleep. Sitting up, head-splitting, I answered the phone.

"Uh, Dan Lewis," I mumbled. "Who—"

"Dan?"

"Cassie?"

I couldn't believe it.

"My god, how are you? I've been trying—"

"It's all fucked, Dan. Everything is fucked."

"What do you mean?"

A deep, sinking pit opened in my belly. This was it, the call I had been dreading.

"You have to come and get me. Please, Dan, *you have to come and get me out of here.*"

"Okay, okay, calm down."

"It's too late! Those videos...they were all *true*." She was sobbing, hysterical.

"What videos? What are you talking about?"

"It grows inside you...it incubates, that's what I heard

one of the nurses say. Oh god, it might be inside me *right now!*"

"Cassie!"

I never shouted at her. Never. But at that moment, it was all I could do. I didn't want our last moments together to be like this. "Listen, they won't let me in. If the cops see me on the street, they'll send me home."

"Everything's gone to hell, Dan! Don't you see? Don't you understand? The virus is alive…it's been using us as a host!"

I'm not ashamed to admit I broke down. To hear the woman you loved, your best friend, lose her mind…I doubt there's any torment on Earth as bad as that.

"The blood…it's the blood," she said, but she sounded distant. A sharp *bang* rang out down the phone.

"Cassie? What was that?" It sounded like a gunshot. Another followed, then screaming, a woman screaming.

"Guns don't work," she said, and she was crying too. "Come and get me, Dan. I need to be with you. I don't think I can face it alone."

"I'll be there," I said. "I promise."

"I love you," she said.

"I love you too."

Another gunshot, and then the phone went dead. I stared at it for what may as well have been forever, then swung my legs out of bed, my body tense. The apartment felt empty without her, and I grabbed her pillow, held it to my face, breathing in the lingering scent of her hair, her perfume. I hadn't changed the sheets since she…left. Hadn't done much, all things told, except drink. I wasn't living…I was existing, and not even doing that very well.

Cassie was my everything. I didn't feel complete without her. Yeah, I know that's cheesy, but what can I say, I'm a sentimental guy.

At least then I was a sentimental guy with purpose.

I had to get to Cassie.

---

I threw on jeans and a shirt, head swimming with a mixture of confusion, despair, and a hangover. The police sirens wailed their doleful, sad song. It sounded like there were hundreds of them, driving all across the city.

It was a dangerous time to travel.

If they caught me, they would ask to see my papers. We were only allowed to remain within our small district, except for emergencies. Any time I left the house, I had to carry my papers with me to show what area I should be in. Failure to comply meant a hefty fine and a possible jail sentence, and at the rate the virus was spreading through our penal system, it was a literal death sentence.

But where was I right now, if not in my own personal prison?

As I laced up my shoes, I wondered if I could get a taxi. I tried calling, but the line was dead.

"Shit," I said. There had to be a faster way to get to the hospital. It would take me at least an hour on foot. But by car, and with the streets as empty as they were, I could make the journey in minutes. Of course, it was all moot, because I didn't actually *have* a car. But I knew someone who did...

Charles Napier.

He lived upstairs, with his wife Netta. He was a good man, and one of the only neighbors we had gotten to know and like. Most people round here kept to themselves, put their heads down when you passed them, but Charles and Netta threw barbecues every summer, and invited the whole block. He had a car, a beat-up old Honda that was one trip away from the scrap heap.

But it would get me to the hospital, if — and it was a big if — he would let me have it.

That was it. Decision made. I grabbed my keys and phone, and left the apartment Cassie and I had shared for three years without looking back.

The stairwell was quiet, as it should be at seven in the morning. My footsteps shattered the peace as I jogged up the stairs. It was my first real exercise since Cassie had fallen sick, and I felt it from my head to my feet, my poor, aching limbs crying out for mercy. By the time I reached Charles' door, I was out of breath. I waited a second before knocking, composing myself, but thinking of Cassie, and the way she had sounded on the phone.

Scared. Terrified. But not, oddly enough, *sick*.

I rapped my knuckles off the door, and it groaned open.

"Charles?" I said, trying to shout quietly, if that was even possible. I didn't like this. Something was very wrong. Pushing the door open further, I stepped inside. The first thing that hit me was the smell. It was like spoiled meat sizzling on the sidewalk on a scorching summer day. "Charles? Netta? Anyone home? It's Dan. Dan Lewis."

No answer.

I walked into the narrow hallway. Unlike our place, which eternally looked like a frat house, The Napiers' apartment was lived in. Photos of their family lined the walls, compared to the one poster of *Guardians of the Galaxy* that Cassie had put up to bring a bit of color to our bare, cream walls. I always wanted her to hang some of her paintings — they were terrific, even if sometimes I didn't understand them — but she refused, said she didn't want to be influenced by her past work. I didn't understand that either, but I'm no artist, never will be.

The door closed behind me, and I jumped. Something had me spooked. I kept thinking about Cassie, and what she had said.

*The videos...they were all true.*
*It grows inside you...it incubates.*
What did it mean?

"Charles? I need your help." I said, and I noticed an inexplicable tremor in my voice. What if he was dead? And Netta too? I had never seen a dead body before...and never wanted to.

There were two doors at the end of the hall. One led to the kitchen and living room, the other to the bedroom and bathroom. I chose the kitchen. The door swung open on squeaking hinges, and there was Charles. Or at least, I think it was. Bile rose in my throat. He was — for lack of a better term — inside out, like he had swallowed a hand grenade and exploded. His torso was split from gullet to naval, huge flaps of loose skin sagging over the arms of the chair he sat in, surrounded by an enormous pool of blood. I took a step closer, covering my nose and mouth. Blood coated the walls in all directions, dribbling feebly down to the carpet, but his internal organs were gone. I moved closer then stopped, suddenly afraid.

*The blood...it's the blood.*

It seemed to be coming towards me.

I stepped back, bumped into the door. No, it was a mistake...a trick. Regardless, my fingers found the handle, and I let myself back into the hall. It was then I heard the noise, a low, crunchy, chewing sound from behind the bedroom door.

Someone was still alive in there.

"Netta?"

No answer.

My shaking hand found the door, turning the handle slowly, so slowly. It clicked, and opened. The room was dark, the curtains drawn. My eyes adjusted, and I could make out a black shape on the bed. It looked small, like a child.

It was eating something.

Despite every fiber of my being urging me to leave, I groped for the light switch.

The thing on the bed noticed me. It sat up, turning to face me with eyes that seemed to pulse a deep, unnatural yellow.

"Netta?" I said. It was a stupid thing to say. I knew it then, and I know it now.

The thing with the yellow eyes hissed, and then leaped straight for me.

I threw myself to the side, and it smacked hard into the wooden door, smashing through one of the panels. Light from the hallway streamed in, and I caught a fleeting view of the unthinkable madness in the room with me. It had gray skin, lurid neon veins streaking across the twisted, gnarled face. I didn't know what it was, but this much I can say — it wasn't fucking human.

It came at me on its hands and legs, scuttling over the floor, and I scrambled backwards, nowhere to run, nowhere to hide. It jumped again, springing towards me, teeth bared, sinking its foul claws into my shoulders. Hot blood ran down my arms as its teeth gnashed inches from my face. I stumbled back, struggling to keep the creature at bay, tangling myself in the curtains. It shrieked an awful, gut-wrenching wail, so loud that my ears rang, and for a moment I could hear nothing but my heartbeat, loud and heavy. I pulled away in terror, and felt something break against the back of my head. I hoped it wasn't my skull.

Thank Christ it was the window.

*The window!*

It was my only chance. The thing kept biting and tearing at my flesh, my arms tiring. I let the creature come closer, drawing my elbows in but keeping my head out of the way, and then spun. Suddenly daylight blinded me, and I faced the window, the creature pressed up against it. I pushed as hard as I could, the window shattering, but the misshapen freak in my arms didn't let go, digging its claws in further. I roared in pain, and put my hand on its throat. The skin was hard, leathery. My other hand reached for the remains of the window, the thick shards of glass that remained in the frame. I snapped one off, slicing through my palm, and thrust it into the creature's eyeball. The juicy orb burst, foamy yellow liquid oozing from the ruptured organ. The thing shrieked again, but its grip had lessened, and I shoved it once more, aware that I was right in front of a broken window on the eighth floor of a high rise.

This time, the creature was unprepared.

It sailed through the window, and that was when I saw it, and I mean *really* saw it.

It was short, roughly four-foot-tall, with dark, rough skin. Its naked body was hairless, and covered in those pulsing, grotesque veins, bright reds and blues and yellows. They erupted from the skin like the roots of a tree.

I watched it sail through the air, unsure whether it had four legs, or two arms and two legs, as it shrank to the size of an ant, before landing on the roof a parked car. The glass exploded outwards as the roof dented, and I stood alone in the Napiers' apartment, blood pouring down my arms. I said the only thing that made sense to say.

"What the *fuck* was that?"

## 6

I backed away from the window.

Even at this height, there was no wind, no cooling breeze. The heat invaded the room like an intruder, light streaming in. I turned towards the door, and there was sweet old Netta on the bed. The creature had torn her to shreds. Her face was mangled, the white bone of her skull visible through the mutilations. Her throat had been torn out. I looked as close as I dared, and saw teeth marks. They dotted her body. The poor woman was in her nightgown, one leg missing from below the knee, the stump red and raw from gnawing teeth.

I vomited.

I couldn't help it. My legs went weak, and I crumbled to the floor.

What *was* that thing? Where had it come from? It had killed Charles, and then Netta. Or had it?

*It grows inside you...it incubates.*

No, that couldn't be right. It wasn't possible. It was the absolute goddam motherfucking *opposite* of possible. Okay, so the creature looked a lot like the ones in the videos...but they were fake. They were special effects. This...this was real.

I got to my feet, slumping against the wall, and took a step forwards. You want the truth? You want the god's honest truth about everything that happened? Fine, I'll give it to you. I stepped in my vomit, and I slipped and landed on my ass. For a while there, I wasn't sure if I was gonna get up or not.

But then I remembered Cassie. Her phone call. The fear in her voice. The gunshots. The mutations.

It was all coming together, and the realization chilled me to my fucking marrow. That *thing* was it. That was the mutation of the virus. It had burst out of Charles Napier, and murdered his wife.

Eaten her.

And it would have done the same to me. Would that happen to everyone who carried the virus? Was that what would happen to—

I got to my feet and stormed from the bedroom, heading for the door. The house-keys dangled from a little metal hook in the hallway, and next to *them?* You guessed it.

The car keys.

I shoved them in my pocket. Then — because somehow my brain was still functioning — I wandered into the kitchen and grabbed the biggest fucking knife I'd ever seen. I felt the weight of it. No, I wanted something more substantial. Discarding the knife, I entered the living room.

There, above the television, was Charles Napier's prize possession — a 1955 New York Yankees commemorative baseball bat, engraved with the names of the championship winning team. On long drunken nights before all this happened, before it all began, Charles would sometimes take that bat down and show it to me, let me handle it.

Honestly, I've never been much of a baseball fan, but I made sure to show respect to that bat. It meant a lot to Charles. I looked at him, sitting there, split open like a gutted fish.

"I hope you don't mind," I said, swinging the bat, listening to the immensely satisfying *whoosh* as it cut through the air like a rotor-blade. He just stared up at the ceiling, with blank, expressionless eyes.

"I gotta go get Cassie," I said. "She needs me. I'm gonna borrow your car too." I waited a moment, as if expecting a response. I don't know why — like I said, there's a respect you've gotta have, whether it's for people or their things. Without that, we're all just punks on the street.

I didn't think he'd mind. Charles had always liked Cassie, and she looked up to him like a father. She had never known hers, and mine was a deadbeat alcoholic, so Charles was the closest to a father figure in both our lives.

I left without another word. I had said all I needed to say. My mind was a whirlwind as I left the apartment. From far below a woman screamed. The elevator was still on my level, so I got in and hit B. The basement was the parking garage, and there I would find Charles' Honda. The doors slid shut, and I gripped the bat tighter. In the movies, that was always when the monster attacked, just as the doors were closing.

Not this time.

They shut silently, and then the elevator was moving. I relaxed a little, safe in the narrow confines of the elevator. Cassie was the claustrophobic of the two. She hated the elevator, tried never to use it unless someone was in there with her.

Cassie.

I hoped she was okay. Hell, she should be. I had dealt

with one, and I'm hardly a tough guy. Sure, it had clawed me good, and nearly taken my face off, but I had handled it.

But how many patients were in the hospital with the virus? Hundreds? Thousands? And what if they were all harboring some creature?

What if Cassie was?

The thought knocked the wind outta me. If I hadn't already spewed, I would've done it again, and left a nice little present for the next occupant. The elevator pinged, and I readied myself to get out.

But it wasn't at the basement yet. It was Level Two.

The doors opened.

7
―――

I HAD NEVER FELT ANYTHING LIKE IT.

At least, not at the opening of an elevator door.

Years back, I was on a date with this girl I met at the gym. It was going well, we were hitting it off. I walked her home, thinking all the way back about whether or not to kiss her, when this bum came shambling out of a parking lot towards us. We tried to ignore him, but he pulled a gun. I don't know where he got it from, or why he hadn't pawned it yet, but when I stared down that barrel I swear I almost pissed myself. The fucker robbed me blind, my girl too. I didn't call her again, to save us both the embarrassment.

That was how I felt as the doors slid electronically open, and a long shadow fell across the inside of the elevator. At first I thought no one was getting in, and I tapped the B button rapidly.

"Hold the door."

Dammit.

I sighed. An old lady entered, leaning on a cane. Could she not hurry up? I knew I was being unreasonable, but I had somewhere to be.

"Level one," she said. She glared at me in distrust, her skin pale and wrinkled, but her eyes sharp. "You need a doctor?" she said, eyeing up my blood-soaked shirt sleeves.

"I'm heading to the hospital."

"You don't have that virus, do you?"

"I don't think bleeding shoulders is a symptom."

She shook her head in disgust. "Rude *and* ugly."

I ignored her. Hell, I was barely listening. I wanted to grab her, shake her, tell her what I had seen…but what *had* I seen? In the ensuing minutes, it seemed to get less and less real, to the point where I was questioning what had actually happened. That might sound ridiculous, but it was more plausible than some virus-spawned monster bursting out of a grown man's stomach and eating his wife.

Shit, I couldn't let her out there. I had to try.

"Listen lady, you going outside?"

"What's it to you?" Typical New Yorker.

I tried to find the right words. "There's…something going on. The virus, it's—"

"What about it?"

Christ, how long did this elevator take?

"It's more dangerous than before. More contagious."

"Son, I've lived through the depression, more wars than I can remember, and six husbands." The bell pinged and the doors opened. "If I wanna go outside, I'm not gonna let some piss-weasel disease—"

The creature threw itself into the elevator, its jaws clamping down hard on the old woman's face. I drew back the baseball bat, but there was no room to swing.

It bit down, those massive teeth shredding her loose skin. I dropped the bat and grabbed the creature, and it lashed out with a ragged claw, the air rippling in front of me. The woman staggered out of the elevator, her cries muffled by the monster that hung from her face. Blood gushed wildly, getting in my eyes. I wiped it away, but the elevator doors were already closing. Through the gap, I saw the woman fall to her knees. The creature's jaws clamped shut, a vice squeezing a ripe tomato, and then the doors closed.

I stood in shocked silence.

Was that the creature I had thrown from the window?

No, it had both its eyes. This was another one. A *different* one. My heart sank. There's only so long you can deny the truth, especially when it's biting the faces off elderly ladies right in front of you.

"As the old saying goes," I whispered.

I looked at myself in the mirrored wall, and saw a man I didn't recognize. He was frightened, older. Bloodier, for sure. I shoulda washed. Out on the streets, I would look pretty damn conspicuous, my face and shirt drenched in blood.

Don't worry, officer, it's not *all* mine.

That woman was dead. I had gone from having never seen a dead body, to seeing three in the space of five minutes. I figured that by the end of the day, I'd have seen a hell of a lot more.

The elevator stopped, and I warily got out, holding onto the baseball bat so hard my knuckles whitened. Woe betide any fucker planning on sneaking up on *me*. I'd give them a face full of wood.

Wait, I just heard that.

Let me try again.

Woe betide any fucker planning on sneaking up on *me*. I'd smash their face so hard, they'd be picking teeth out of their ears for days.

Yeah, that was better, the sort of thing a drill sergeant would say, or Arnold Schwarzenegger. Nah, he'd say something like *home run*, after hitting someone in the face with a baseball bat.

I was getting sidetracked, and no wonder. My mind was struggling to process what was happening. I had to concentrate, focus on one thing.

Cassie.

Oh, and the car. So, *two* things. I could deal with that. Once I found the car, I could forget about it, and focus on Cassie.

The doors wheezed shut, and I faced the garage. Cars lined the walls, and I looked for the distinctive dented fender of the Honda. I hadn't driven in a decade — in this city, you don't need to — and I hoped I could remember how to do it.

The lights above me flickered, because of course they fucking did. I wanted to throw my bat at them, destroy them, but I was angry, not stupid.

The Honda jutted out from the rest of the cars, right at the back of the lot. I thought I heard something behind me, and spun, bat at the ready, resting on my shoulder.

Nothing.

At least, nothing I could see. I pressed a hand to my wounds. The bleeding had stopped, the cuts not as deep as I'd feared.

I resumed my journey, painfully aware of how alone I was. For the first time in my life, I wished I owned a firearm. I'd always figured I didn't need one, because I had no plans to shoot up a school anytime soon, but I hadn't foreseen an invasion by...what? What were those things? Monsters? Aliens?

Would we ever know?

Something dripped on my head. Startled, I looked up, ready to peer into the eyes of one of those creatures. A cracked pipe leaked cold, foul-smelling liquid onto my face. It rolled down my cheek like a tear, and I wiped it away and moved on.

It occurred to me that in all the confusion, I hadn't tried to phone Cassie back. I checked my phone. The number she had called from was listed as unknown, and when I tried to ring, it wouldn't let me. Dammit. Her own phone was still in our apartment. If she only had it with her, we could have spoken every day.

If only.

What if.

No point in dwelling on shit like that. That way lay madness.

I reached the Honda and stuck the keys in the lock. It opened, and I got in. It was almost too easy. The car didn't start on the first try, nor the second. Maybe it was the car's fault, maybe it was my own. Like I said, I hadn't been behind the wheel for a while. Thankfully, it was a case of third time lucky, and the old engine finally growled into life. Light spilled into the garage, and I noticed the elevator doors were opening again. I gunned the engine, taking off, scraping the side of the Honda against a BMW, metal grinding against metal.

There was no time to leave a note.

"Sorry," I muttered, and drove through the gauntlet of cars to the exit ramp.

That was what I saw the woman.

I braked sharply, throwing myself forward. She came towards me, wearing a vest and yoga pants, running for her life, her bare feet slapping off the concrete. She was covered — and I mean *covered* — in blood. I waited, the engine idling. There was movement behind her, and I knew instantly what it was. I pressed the accelerator and the vehicle shot forwards, slowing as I neared the woman. She drew level and threw the door open, so hard I thought it might tear free from the car.

She jumped in.

"Drive!" she shouted, slamming the door. I saw the creature racing towards us on all fours, the flickering lights creating a nightmarish strobing effect. "Fucking drive!"

She didn't need to tell *me* twice.

Actually, I suppose she just did.

Fuck it.

The car jerked forwards. The creature was between us and the exit, the collision unavoidable. No problem. I would splatter the little fucker all across the garage. At the last second it leaped, crashing into the windshield, the glass spider-webbing, obscuring my vision. The woman screamed, and I think I did too. Through the fractured glass I could see its face. It, too, was coated in dripping gore. It raised a clawed fist and hammered on the glass.

"Oh god, oh god," the woman kept shouting, as if that fucking helped.

Splinters of razor sharp glass showered our laps, the creature reaching one scaly hand in, groping just in front of the woman's chest. With my right hand, I fumbled for the seat recline switch, found it, and pulled it. Her seat fell backwards out of reach, and she screamed again, as the creature resumed pummeling the windshield. We were almost at the exit ramp.

The red and white barrier was down.

Unable to raise it, I slammed my foot to the pedal, trying to look past the creature, spinning the wheel, aiming for the barrier.

"Cover your face," I barked at the woman. Despite her panic, she did as I told her, and seconds later the Honda hit the barrier. The metal struck the creature in the back, slicing it in two, before hitting the windshield. The screen shattered, and I was promptly showered in broken glass and creature guts. Its blood was yellow, pustulent, but I had little time to register it. The barrier snapped, and then we were up the ramp and on the street, the tires screeching as I jerked the wheel. I noticed flashing lights, heard a siren. To my right, I saw a cop car heading straight for us. Acting purely on instinct, I turned the vehicle the other way. We hit a parked car, and came to a stop.

The cops drove past. As they did, I glimpsed an officer in the driver's seat, one of the creatures on top of him, clawing at the bloody mask of his face. They accelerated away. They must have been doing at least ninety when they hit the apartment block down the street. A colossal, deafening roar rang out through the streets, as the cop car folded in on itself like an accordion.

"What's happening?"

The woman. I had forgotten all about her. I looked at her, lying practically horizontal, and grabbed the seat, pulling it level with my own. Her top half was drenched in blood, while her legs were soaked in the sticky yellow goo from the creature. Her wide eyes were like two boiled eggs on a red plate.

"I don't know," I said honestly. "I just...don't know."

"My brother...he..." she looked like she was grappling with her sanity.

"It's okay," I said. "You don't need to tell me."

"I have to tell someone, or else I think I'll go crazy."

"We might already be," I said, and I wasn't joking. I knew we had to get going, I had to find Cassie, but right now, I wasn't capable of driving. My legs trembled, my hands shook, and my mind was a blur. I needed to, if not *relax*, then at least compose myself. There were only so many times you could almost die in a morning before the mental toll became too much.

"My neighbor," I said. "I went up to see him. This is his car. There was something wrong. The door was unlocked. I went inside, and found one of those...*things*. It had eaten—"

"They come from inside," she said, sounding slightly calmer than before. "From inside...people. Haven't you seen the videos?"

"Yeah. I thought..."

"They were fake."

"That's right. When there's so much bullshit out there, so many lies, it's hard to tell fact from fiction."

"That's what my brother said. I've been staying with him during the lockdown. He's got...problems. Mental health stuff, y'know. I didn't want to leave him alone. I was worried. Then he got sick..."

"He go to hospital?"

She shook her head. "He didn't want to. He was terrified of hospitals." She looked at me imploringly. "He wasn't that bad! Just a cough and a fever. He was breathing okay. We both stayed in, had our groceries delivered...it was fine. Everything was normal. Then last night..."

"What happened?"

She stared out the window, watching smoke billow from the police car. Elsewhere, sirens blared again. They never stopped anymore.

"He got worse. Much worse. He looked like shit. I remember thinking it looked like something was eating him from the inside." She fixed me with a stare, hazel eyes blazing. She couldn't have been more than twenty. "Turns out I was right," she said.

"What happened?"

She sighed. "Don't you have somewhere to go?"

"Yes. But not yet. I don't…I don't feel up to it." I tried to smile. "Hey, we're not doing a great job of social distancing, are we?"

"I think it's a little late for that," she said quietly. She took my hand. It was the first time I had touched another human since Cassie was taken to hospital. It felt so good I wanted to cry.

"I'm Dan," I said.

"Apple."

"Like the phone?"

"Like the *fruit*," she corrected. Then, conspiratorially, she whispered "I don't wanna get sued."

I laughed. It sounded unnatural. But what was natural anymore?

"It came out of my brother," she said. "It had been in there all along, growing, using him as a host. I heard him screaming this morning. I knew what was coming. I'd seen the videos, and unlike him — and you, I guess — I believed them. When the president said they were fake, that was the moment I knew it was all real." A tear formed in the corner of her eye, and she tried to blink it away. It trickled down her cheek, carving a path through the quickly-drying blood.

"What did you do?"

"He had a gun. He asked me…he *begged* me to kill him. I couldn't do it. I…I left him…I locked him in his room, with the gun. When he started to scream again, I ran. I didn't know where, didn't even care. I just had to get away." She looked at me again, with those big, wet eyes. "I never heard the gunshot," she said.

"So who's blood is that?" I asked, keeping my voice low and soft.

She touched her face, as if she hadn't realized she was soaked in the stuff.

"I don't know who he was. A neighbor, I guess."

I nodded, letting her speak.

"He was just standing on the stairs. An old man...he looked lost. I thought he had dementia. When I got closer, I could hear something dripping. There was blood on the floor. He moved, twitching, and then he just started...shaking, all over. I thought he was having a fit, so I touched him, and he felt..."

She stopped, letting the statement hang in the air.

"Felt what?"

"He felt soft. Like there was nothing inside, no bones, no muscle. Like a bag of water. And then the bag burst..."

She broke down in tears, and I probed no further.

"My wife is in the hospital," I said. "I'm going to go get her."

She said not a word, but I could see it in her face.

She thought it was hopeless.

"We don't know how bad is out there," I said, trying to convince myself. "I've killed two of those things already."

"Yeah," she said. "But what if there were two at the same time? Or more? How many do you think will be in the hospital?"

"I'm trying *not* to think about that."

She looked at the baseball bat beside me. "At least you came prepared."

I turned the key, and engine started first time. "I have to go," I said, looking straight ahead. "I love her. It might be the last time I see her."

"I understand."

"She phoned me about a half hour ago. She's still alive."

"Was she sick...with the virus?"

I knew what she was getting at. "She's not carrying one of those things. She sounded fine on the phone."

Apple nodded. Such a strange name.

"Okay," she said.

I reversed the car, pulling onto the quiet road again. "Is there anywhere I can drop you?"

"I've got nowhere to go," she said.

"Wanna stick with me for a while?"

"Sure."

It was good enough for me.

I didn't want to be alone right now.

# PART II

Thoughts and Fuckin' Prayers

## 8

THE STREETS WERE QUIET.

We passed a few civilians, wandering aimlessly like lost souls, some queuing outside stores and pharmacies, others walking their dogs. Cop cars raced by several times, but they paid us scant attention, their sirens a near-constant soundtrack.

We didn't speak. What was there to say? The whole world was ending before our eyes. I swerved the car to avoid a body in the road. It had fallen from a window, the brains splattered across the tarmac. The closer we got to the center, to the hospital, the more bodies we saw. Most were lying there wide open, little bloody footprints leading away from them, though the creatures kept to the darkness.

Most of the time.

Sometimes I would catch a glimpse out of the corner of my eye, something lurking in the long shadows cast by the early morning sun. As we drove, a cool wind blew in through the broken windshield, keeping the heat at bay for a little while. Once, a man ran out in front of the car wearing nothing but a towel.

"They're coming!" he shouted, hammering his fists off the hood. "They're coming!"

"We're really fucked this time, aren't we?" said Apple, as the man hurried off to harass another car, his towel falling off as he ran.

"Looks like it."

We drove on. Apple took out her phone.

"It's happening everywhere," she said.

"What are you looking at?"

"Twitter. The news doesn't seem to be covering it, and when they do, they're just calling it the Chinese Hoax."

"What's President Asshole saying?"

"Something about thoughts and prayers. Oh wait, now he's saying it's the media wanting to boost their falling ratings. And also a bio-weapon from China. He says North Korea is the only country doing things right."

"Pretty on-brand," I said. We weren't far from the hospital. There were more people out, more vehicles on the road. We arrived at a small tailback of cars.

"Why've we stopped?" said Apple. She sounded nervous.

I didn't know, so I opened my door. She grabbed my arm. "Be careful."

I nodded. "I will."

I got out, looking around for anything suspicious, seeing nothing out of the ordinary. Well, apart from the upside down van in the middle of the road. Someone beeped their horn at it, steam billowing from the upturned vehicle.

"Yeah, that'll help," I said.

Another car, going the other direction, had driven into it, and the road was at an impasse. I got back in. "Have to go a different way," I said, reversing. I bumped into the car behind me, and they honked their horn angrily. Soon, all the cars joined in, an unending cacophony of noise.

*The Blood Beast Mutations*

Someone in an apartment leaned out their window and yelled at us.

For one second, everything felt normal again.

I navigated us out, and after a five-point turn, headed back the way we had come, taking the first left down a narrow street. It was a minor diversion, and wouldn't add more than a few minutes to the trip. I wondered what Apple planned to do when we got to the hospital, but I daren't ask her.

"Dan, look," she said, pointing.

One of the creatures on the sidewalk, its face buried between the legs of a corpse. It ripped a chunk out of their crotch, blood streaming in a wide arc from the wound. It chewed and swallowed, then returned for more. The person's fingers still moved, dancing out a beat on the concrete. I subconsciously sped up, wanting to get past the nightmarish tableaux. The creature spotted us and started towards the car. I pressed the accelerator as it gave chase, its gray legs blurring.

I didn't slow down, not even after we'd left it far behind.

We turned a corner, then another, gradually making our way to the hospital, the engine of the old Honda chugging along nicely. We passed more of the creatures, too many, some of them trying to keep up with us for a while before giving up and going in search of easier prey.

As long as we were in the car, and moving, we were safe.

"What's that ahead?" said Apple.

The sun was in my eyes. "I don't see...*shit*." I slammed the brakes. Hundreds of figures were coming towards us, black shapes moving through the streets.

*"USA, USA, USA,"* they chanted.

"Protestors," I said, grimly.

"Will they let us through?"

"I don't think so."

"We could park," suggested Apple, "and hide in the car, wait for them to pass."

"There's a lot of them. If they see us hiding, they'll..."

"They'll what?"

"Let's go another way," I said, not wanting to think about it.

I put the car in reverse and checked the rear-view mirror. My heart stopped. More protestors coming the other way.

"Shit. We're trapped."

Apple looked over her shoulder. "Oh god, oh god," she said, over and over again. She knew as well as I did that if you weren't with the protestors, you were against them, and the consequences were deadly. There were reports of violence all over the country. It started as verbal abuse and intimidation. Then it had progressed to humiliation. The protestors would target people wearing face masks, strip them naked, and force them to walk the streets in nothing but their masks. Then the beatings had begun, followed by the rapes, the killings, the shootings, the—

Gunshots rang out, machine guns, assault rifles, bullets piercing the air.

*"USA, USA, USA."*

They were closing in. We had to decide, and fast.

"Get out," I said, grabbing my baseball bat. "This is a residential area. Someone's gotta help us."

Together, we ran to the nearest door and started buzzing the names. The whole country was on lockdown — someone *had* to be in.

"No one's answering," said Apple.

"Try some more!"

I jabbed at the buttons, frantic now. We were right in the

middle. A shot fired, the bullet ricocheting off the wall nearby. They had seen us.

"Run!" I shouted, racing to Apple and grabbing her arm. We pounded down the sidewalk, bullets whizzing by.

They weren't protestors anymore — they were a goddam militia. Some of them ran after us, discarding their signs. I noticed a pharmacy, and dragged Apple towards it. The door opened and a worried looking man peered out, checking up and down the street. He saw us coming and ran back inside, slamming the door.

"Wait!" I shouted. I could see him locking it through the glass.

I let go of Apple and shifted the bat into my right hand, swinging it as I ran, bringing it down hard on the glass door. It exploded inwards, and we barged inside.

"What are you doing?" said the owner. "My fucking door! You'll goddam pay for that, you—"

"You got a back door?" I shouted, taking him by the lapel and pulling him towards me. "Another exit?"

"Fuck you," said the man, his nostrils flaring in indignation. Now, I'm not a violent guy, but desperate times call for fucking head-butts. His nose crunched juicily against my forehead, and I asked him again.

"Back door?"

He gestured with his thumb, and I let him go. He crumpled to the floor, wiping the blood that flowed down his chin.

"Come on," I said to Apple.

"I hope they get you," said the man. "I hope they kill you and rape your bitch."

As Apple passed, she punched him hard in the face, which shut him up. I wanted to crush his skull. He would tell them where we went, and they would follow. Why? I didn't know. For something to do, to feel like real men, whatever excuse they were using to terrorize the city when America was already on its knees.

We ran behind the counter, leaving the worker licking his wounds, and hurtled through a door into a stock room.

"Where's the way out?" I cried.

"Did he trick us?"

I checked down various aisles. Shelves lined with stock, a fire extinguisher, cardboard boxes...all useless. We were trapped. That bastard had—

"Dan, over here!"

I ran towards her voice. Down the last aisle was a fire exit, boxes stacked in front of it. She was already tearing them down. The bullets were so loud it was like they were in the store, and who knows, maybe they were? While Apple cleared a path, I ran back to the stock room door and slammed it shut. Then, I grabbed some of the boxes from the shelves, using them to wedge the door.

"Dan, come on!"

Something hit the door. The boxes buckled, but held... for now. They weren't heavy, and I doubted they'd last long.

"We're gonna get you!" shouted one of the protestors, as I ran to Apple. She had the door open, and we made it outside.

"They're over here," shouted another voice. Two men stood at the end of the street, pointing at us, rifles slung over their shoulders. Jesus, I just wanted to get to Cassie!

Was that too much to fucking ask?

I scanned the area and spotted a fire escape leading up to the roof. There was a padlock on it — the fire safety guys obviously hadn't been round to check this place in a long time — and I did the one thing I could think to do. I brought the bat down hard on the lock. The rusted metal broke on impact, clanging to the ground.

"This way," I said to Apple. I let her go first, as the protestors made their way down the street.

"What do they want?" she said, which was exactly what I was thinking. I didn't have an answer for her. She raced up the metal stairway, and I was close behind. I looked to see if they were following. They were. Just a couple of 'em, but enough to cause me to freak out internally.

In my head, they caught up with us, held us down, and then the leader would walk up to me, extend his hand, and say, *hey, you dropped your wallet, mister. Here you go. Have a nice day!*

Doubtful. We were living in the worst possible timeline, the one with the fucking murder hornets. Yeah, I know I keep bringing them up, but come on…could they not have waited? One biblical plague per year was more than enough.

"Where are we going?" shouted Apple. She didn't sound out of breath yet, and I was stunned, because I could hardly fuckin' breathe, and I wasn't even thirty yet.

"The roof," I said, which was a poor answer, but all I had. Honestly, I was all out of ideas, apart from one word that flashed before my eyes like a neon sign.

SURVIVE

## 9

WE MADE IT TO THE ROOF.

I don't know what I hoped to find up there, but whatever it was, it was in short supply. It was just a fucking *roof*. No doors, no nothing. I looked over the edge of the building. Man, we were high up. If this was a movie, I would have taken Apple's hand, and we would have jumped into a convenient pile of garbage bags. But unless we wanted to take a swan dive face-first onto the sidewalk, we had to come up with something different. At least we had a head-start — their guns must have been slowing them down. We ran across the rooftop, Apple taking the lead.

"There," she shouted.

Ho-lee shit, she was right. A skylight, dead ahead. Our luck was finally in. I glanced over my shoulder. Those guys were still huffing their way up the fire escape. We had time. Not a lot, but enough. Apple got there first, peering in while I panted towards her.

Don't judge me. How much exercise can you really do when you can't leave your apartment?

"It's high," she said. I arrived at the skylight and looked

*The Blood Beast Mutations*

in. She was right. It was a big drop into the penthouse apartment. In the center, about twenty foot below, was a massive kingsize bed. It looked like it was built to take some action, and I sensed this was some sordid love-nest, the kinda place a businessman brings his floozies for a quick, but expensive, fumble.

"How do we get down?" said Apple.

"The old fashioned way," I said. I smashed the glass with the bat, and mentally thanked Charles Napier for his services. One day, if all this came to an end and things returned to normal, I would head to the cemetery with a bottle of Johnnie Walker and pour one out for the old man. I owed him.

"Okay, you go first," I said. Apple looked unsure. I couldn't blame her. It *was* high. "There's no time for this," I said. "They're on their way."

"I don't think I can do it. What if I miss?"

There was no time to argue.

"Okay, *I'll* go first, and catch you."

"You mean that?"

"Fuck, of course!"

She nodded resolutely. "Then jump."

I smacked the bat against the skylight once more for luck, dislodging a few pieces of glass. I hoped they weren't falling onto the bed, but there was nothing I could do if they were.

"Here goes," I muttered, stepping off into the void. I left my stomach behind, somewhere up on the roof, and plummeted, bending my knees, braced for impact. I hit the mattress, and sprung halfway across the room, a heavy wooden wardrobe breaking my fall. Did I say breaking my fall? I meant damn near breaking my fucking *neck*.

"You okay?" Apple shouted from above.

I dusted myself off, trying my best to look unfazed, and gave her a thumbs-up like some half-assed eighties superhero.

"Ready when you are," I shouted, preparing to catch her in case she bounced off the bed and went flying like I did. A gunshot rattled my eardrums. I looked up at Apple. "Come on!"

She didn't move. She just stood there, rocking on her heels.

"Apple, hurry!"

She toppled forwards, her head cracking off the skylight frame. I scrambled over the bed, but I was too slow. I had expected her to overshoot the landing. She landed on her shoulder, and something snapped, but it didn't matter. By then it was too late. The bloody crater in the back of her head told me she had been dead before she broke her neck. I saw shadows approaching through the skylight, and ducked into the darkness, out of sight.

*"I got her, Junior. I fucking got her!"* one of them said. My grip on the bat tightened.

*"Where'd the other one go?"*

*"Down there."*

*"Then let's go!"*

I shuffled further into the corner of the room. I couldn't let them see me. They had guns, for christ's sake. What use was a baseball bat against an assault rifle?

One of the men yelled as his body sailed through the air. He landed on the bed, and I waited for it to propel him onwards. Instead, the frame collapsed, the mattress cushioning his fall.

That had to have been one thick, expensive mattress.

*"You fucking broke it, man,"* shouted the guy on the roof.

"Don't be a pussy. Get your ass down here."

*The Blood Beast Mutations*

I could see the man's feet dangling over the edge like a toddler in an adult chair. His chunky legs appeared, and he turned the other way, lowering himself down. I sheltered behind a bureau, the feel of the bat in my hands keeping me sane. The first man looked up at his friend, the sun in his eyes. It was the only thing stopping him from seeing me. If they came to check on Apple, I was fucked.

Poor Apple. I had known her for less than an hour, but already we'd been through a lot together. Her death felt like losing a friend, as crazy as that might sound.

The other man landed clumsily, falling onto his fat ass. The gun spilled from his hand, firing off a shot into the wall.

"Jesus, careful there!"

I got a clear look at them in the sunlight, the kind of good ol' boy jackasses I saw on the news every night, from their red caps to their laced-up combat boots. The first man was older, with a scraggly white beard and a pinched, sour expression. The other guy, though I could only see him from behind, looked younger, and sounded it too. He was a, shall we say, *rounder* gentleman, his voluminous ass quaking as he stood in pants that were so obscenely tight, I could see the outline of his briefs.

"Where'd he go?" said the younger man, picking up his gun with fumbling fingers.

"You almost shot me, Junior."

"You were the one who broke the bed!"

"It was damn-well broken before I landed on it. Too much humpin', likely. And son, for the record, you're in no position to be chastisin' folks about their heaviness."

"What's that supposed to mean?"

The older man shook his head, his beard starched and unmoving. "Boy, if I was being charitable, I would describe you as a fat, ugly son of a bitch. But I'm not. So let me just say—"

"I get it, Pops," snapped Junior. I could see his buttcheeks clench in anger. "Now where'd he go?"

"See that door, son? I find that most people, if they leave a room, they use the door. Now maybe you could just jump up and down until the floor breaks, but you ain't most people, praise Jesus, because there ain't a bicycle on God's green Earth built to take the likes of you."

Junior said nothing. I wondered if Pops was his father, or just some asshole.

"Now quit your jaw-flappin' and follow me." He walked to the door and yanked it open. He didn't even have time to register surprise before the dark gray creature launched itself at his face.

Pops spun, trying to dislodge the beast, but its jaws were fastened shut on his face, claws hacking at his chest like miniature hatchets.

"Oh Jesus, Mary and Joseph," said Junior, walking backwards and tripping over his own feet. Blood erupted from Pops' face, shooting out in thick, scarlet jets, painting the walls. He let go of his his rifle, floundering in dizzying circles.

"Shoot it!" I shouted, but Junior just sat there blubbering like a baby. I had to do something. I ran, picked up Junior's rifle — Jesus, it was so heavy — and aimed it at the creature, which clung to Pops like a parasite. His skull cracked, and he fell to the floor. This was it, my chance. I pulled the trigger, and...nothing. I tried again.

Still nothing.

I looked to Junior, his face a soft, wet ball of dough.

"I only had one bullet left," he said.

The creature raised its head, tearing off the front of the

older man's face. It hung between its jaws, beard and everything. Just the back of Pops' head remained. No eyes, no nose, nothing but a gaping hole crudely held together by shattered bone, blood spilling freely onto the floor. The creature looked from me, to Junior, and back again. I kept the rifle trained on it, wondering what it was thinking. Would it fear me, and leave me alone, or would it regard me as more of a threat, and attack first? Hell, did it even know what a gun was?

"Pops," said Junior, and he crawled blindly towards his friend (father?), oblivious to the lurking danger right in front of his eyes.

"Stay back," I said. "You got a fucking death wish?"

Apparently he did.

He crawled onwards, catching the creature's attention. This one looked slightly bigger than the others I'd seen, it's claws longer, sharper, *deadlier*. Transparent goo dribbled from its mouth, pooling on the floor. It drew back its ghastly, shriveled lips, baring enormous teeth. I didn't know if it could see me or not, as the eyes were yellow orbs, no iris or pupils. I shuffled to my left, and it didn't react. It just stared at the young man, claws lengthening, scratching deep troughs in the wooden floorboards. It was readying itself to pounce, and I took the chance. I tossed the rifle at Junior, shouting, "Catch!" The creature heard me, and I cursed myself for being so stupid. What can I say, I got caught up in the excitement of the moment. The beast spun, but my throw was poor, and the gun smacked it in the face instead.

It wasn't the plan, but it would do.

I dived for Pops' rifle, figuring I'd go into a forward roll and pick the gun up in one slick, well-practised move, rising with the barrel aimed perfectly at the creature's head.

That's not how things work out in real life.

I got the rifle, but slipped for the second time that day, this time in blood rather than vomit. I needed to get some new sneakers, ones with better grip.

I crashed to the ground, facing the wrong way entirely, listening to the desperate screams of the younger man. Pivoting on the floor, I saw the creature was already on him, slashing its claws. At least he was trying to resist, covering his face with arms that were now red-raw and blood-soaked, his camo jacket doing little to protect him. I brought the gun to my shoulder, chafing against my own wounds.

"Hold its head up!" I shouted. I hadn't fired a gun since my college days, and even then my aim had been, quite honestly, terrible. The creature was too close to Junior, and I couldn't fire without possibly hitting him. Mind you, he had no such qualms when pursuing me and Apple over rooftops, guns blazing.

"I don't have a clear shot!"

"Help me," he whimpered, and I circled, trying to find the right angle.

Fuck it.

I strode towards the creature. It turned to me, snarled, and I rammed the barrel into its fucking mouth and squeezed the trigger. The recoil surprised me, the gun almost juddering out of my hands as the back of the creature's head hit the wall fifteen feet away.

"There's another one!" said Junior.

I whirled, finding it in the doorway, and fired again, bullets pumping into its body like rocks dropped into a river from a high bridge. I couldn't stop. The creature's arm flew off squirting thick yellow mucus. A bullet entered its neck, the head lolling to the side. I was losing control of the gun, but I held on, firing until nothing but a puddle of toxic yellow gore remained.

*The Blood Beast Mutations*

The shooting stopped, the rifle out of ammo, yet still I held the trigger, someone somewhere screaming. I realized it was me.

"You got it, you got it," Junior kept saying.

But I didn't stop screaming.

I wanted to, but I couldn't.

## 10

Eventually, I calmed down, placed the weapon on the floor, and retrieved my baseball bat. I didn't look at Junior, didn't say a word. I was strangely embarrassed. I never lost control like that.

Ever.

"What was that thing?" he said softly.

I wasn't sure I owed him an explanation. "Mutation," was all I said.

"Mutation?"

I sighed. "Of the virus. It's changed. It's breeding these... things now."

"The virus is fake," he said. The baseball bat suddenly felt *real* nice in my hands. "It's a hoax."

"Says who?"

"Says the president."

"You believe everything he tells you?"

He nodded eagerly. "He's draining the swamp. Making America great again."

"Yeah, I know, I can read your hat." I looked at him, looked at him *hard*. "You think this is a hoax? Look around you, man! People are dying...thousands of them, *millions*. You know where I'm heading? To the hospital. My fucking wife has this shit. Last time I saw her she couldn't breathe properly, because she was coughing up so much blood. I just want to get to the fucking hospital!" I punctuated the last two words by smacking the wooden bat off the floor. I felt tears coming, and let them fall. "Why are you doing this? Why are you so desperate to force people back to work?"

He looked at his feet. "We have to save the economy," he mumbled.

"An economy ain't worth shit if everyone's dead," I said, and that was the end of that. I left him sitting on the floor, and headed for the door.

Hey, that rhymes.

I was losing it. I had to get out of here. The hospital wasn't far, though without the car, it'd be a good twenty minute jog, and I was tiring fast.

An idea flashed through my mind. Should I go back and break the guy's legs? I should never have told him I was going to the hospital. What if he told his friends? Would they follow me, assuming I had killed old Pops back there?

No, I didn't think he'd do that. I had saved his life. If only I could save the life of every inbred bible-thumping dipshit out there, then maybe they would leave me alone long enough to go and see my wife.

I chuckled coldly. Gallows humor, huh? Whatever gets you through the bad times.

I stepped out into the hallway, hitting the light switch, following the trail of blood left by the creatures. I passed a room where two bodies lay, their stomachs wide open, and kept walking. How many of these things were there? The government had stopped releasing test figures weeks ago, so who knew how many people were infected. Maybe even those who were asymptomatic were hosting those creatures? It was a chilling thought, and I didn't want to dwell on it. At the end of the hall was a door, and I exited the penthouse.

The stair was quiet, and I made my way stealthily down to the first floor. I listened at the door for a while, but I couldn't hear the protestors. Fuck, I mean I couldn't hear the *militia*. Let's call them what they are. A bunch of dumbass shit-stains, who value haircuts over human lives. Opening the door, I peered out, but the street was empty. Time to move.

Spent shells littered the ground as I made my way towards the hospital. In the distance, I could hear them chanting, but it was in the opposite direction. Using my bat like a walking stick, I headed on down the road. I hoped Cassie was safe. But what use was hope right now?

Thoughts and fuckin' prayers had never been enough.

This was a time for action.

## 11

A HELICOPTER BUZZED OVERHEAD.

The sky was swarming with them. I checked my phone. Google reported that my top news story was Topher Grace celebrating his 41$^{st}$ birthday in lockdown. I had no idea who that was. What was it Apple had said? Social media was where the real stories were.

I searched for Twitter. The first result was a series of tweets from the president.

The DEMOCROOKS are doing evil things, BAD things. The Fake News LameStream Media are LYING to the country. Big mistake! I WILL MAKE A LIVE ANNOUNCEMENT TONIGHT!!

Don't believe the hype! If the Chinese Virus was getting worse, I would know about it. I know more about VIRUSES than the do-nothing Democrats. Just ask my Friends at FoxNews. THE COUNTRY WILL REOPEN! THERE WILL BE A VACCINE BY XMAS!!

"Yeah, real presidential," I muttered.

Another copter flew by, this one low enough to ruffle my hair. Most were heading the same direction. Several cop cars raced by, flanking an ambulance. This did not look promising.

Walking on grumbling legs, I turned a corner, and there it was.

The hospital.

All roads leading to it were blocked by armed police. Hundreds of them, as far as I could see. Four copters hovered in the air, snipers aiming from within.

"Cassie," I whispered.

This was it. The epicenter. Ground zero. Well, this and all the other hospitals in the country, but we had been hit hard in New York. Funding was cut, personal protective equipment supplies reassigned to other, more traditionally red states. Our death toll hit eighty-thousand days ago, rocketing up after the president announced an end to the first lockdown.

There were literally thousands — potentially *hundreds* of thousands — of infected people in this state alone. If even half of them were hosting those creatures...even a quarter...

I walked towards the barricades, trying to conceal the bat inconspicuously behind me, and no doubt failing miserably.

"Stop right there, sir," said an officer, his face covered with what looked like an old t-shirt he had fashioned into a makeshift mask. "The hospital is closed."

"My wife's in there," I said.

"I'm sorry, sir. You'll have to go back home."

"I *need* to get in. Please, you don't understand."

"I wish I could help you," he said, and I believed him. "But the whole area is off-limits."

*The Blood Beast Mutations*

"It's those things, isn't it?"

At first the officer said nothing. He lowered his gun, and when he spoke again, the commanding tone of voice was gone. "I don't know what's going on. I just know we can't let anybody in, or out."

"No one out? Not even staff?"

"I'm sorry, man. I really am. My mama's in there, y'know. She doesn't have the virus, she's just sick, like normal sick. I don't know if I'll ever see her again."

I nodded, and turned away. That was it, then. All that effort, and for nothing.

*Nothing.*

It made me want to curl up on the street and go to sleep for a very long time.

"I'm sorry, Cassie," I said. I looked at my phone. No missed calls. There had to be another way in. I could commandeer a copter, or sneak in through the sewers, or...or...

Or not.

I wasn't likely to make my way past hundreds of armed officers, most of whom looked scared shitless. Everybody knew someone who was sick, whether it was family, a friend, a co-worker. It was no longer a case of *my friend's boyfriend's aunt has it*. We had long since bypassed that particular stage.

I had never felt so utterly defeated.

I had failed her. My wife, my love, alone in the hospital, surrounded not just by the infected and the dying, but by blood-thirsty mutants. I looked skyward, and screamed, *"Bring on the murder hornets,"* but even the man in the sky wasn't listening anymore. This was proof that either god was dead, or he hated us so much that he was going to wipe the entire pitiful human race off the face of the planet.

At least things couldn't get any worse.

*"Hey, that's him!"*

I recognized the voice.

*"That's the guy who killed Pops!"*

Wearily, I turned my head towards the sound, and there he was, Junior, the man who's life I had saved only twenty minutes ago. He was pointing at me, gesturing frantically.

*"I told you he was going to the hospital!"*

Bigmouth strikes again. I couldn't keep my trap shut, could I? Just *had* to go and blab my plans to a militant redneck freakshow. Well, now the game was up. I saw them flooding round the corner, a tidal wave of racist aggression and clueless indignation, ten, twenty, fifty, *one hundred* of them, armed and coming towards me. The officers behind me spotted them, a stern voice crackling out over a megaphone.

"Stop right there. This area is off-limits. Please return to where you came from."

It was clear from the way he spoke that he didn't expect them to turn back. The officers had no idea it was me they wanted...they thought they were about to encounter a full-on riot.

And they were.

"Get behind us," said an officer, their guns drawn. The militia advanced. What was it that wrestling commentator used to say...*when the unstoppable force meets the immovable object*...It suddenly occurred to me that Bobby 'The Brain' Heenan had probably not come up with that quote himself. It's funny the way your mind works when you're up shit creek without a paddle.

"I repeat, stay back!" said the officer with the megaphone, but his request went unheeded. A few of the militia members raised their guns and took aim, the officers doing likewise, unprepared for this. They had no riot gear, no body armor. They had expected to keep civilians and journalists from entering the hospital, not to engage in a full-blown street-war.

The tension was thick, oppressive. Officers spoke into radios, helicopters buzzed like flies, fingers itching over triggers, necks slick with sweat.

"What day is it?" one officer asked her colleague.

"Tuesday? Wednesday?" he offered.

She nodded. "We're gonna die, and we don't even know what goddam day it is."

I shuffled through, cops grabbing my arm and hustling me through the crowd to safety, telling me to get out of the way, shoving me closer and closer to the hospital.

I'll never know who fired the first shot, but it split the air like the crack of a whip, and the tension dissipated at once.

Chaos filled the gap.

Someone shouted, people cheered, and an officer next to me crossed himself. The gunfight started. Shots rang out, rattling the windows, bullets zipping by. I had never heard anything like it, the sound of being held against the speakers at a rock concert. My body vibrated, ears ringing, as I made a mad dash towards the hospital.

"Don't go in there," someone said, making no move to stop me. When I turned back, they were lying flat on the ground, a fountain of blood spraying from their ruptured eye socket, a bullet lodged in their skull. The cops were hopelessly outgunned and outnumbered.

It would be a bloodbath.

The snipers took pot-shots at the militia from the vantage point of the copters, but more than a few sniper rifles were required. They needed grenades, a rocket launcher…a fucking bomb.

I jogged to the entrance. It was sealed shut, but that wasn't going to stop me. I hoisted the bat and brought it down hard against one of the glass doors. It cracked, but did not break. I swung again, the bat arcing through the air and smashing the glass, and I stepped inside, the war raging behind me. I didn't know where was safest, outside or in, but I knew I had to find Cassie. Only problem, she could be anywhere. The hospital was *enormous*, and I had never been inside before. Unsurprisingly, bar work doesn't offer much in the way of health insurance. If one of us was sick, we took handfuls of painkillers until the booze numbed the pain.

The lobby was deserted. Red pools of blood covered the floor, smeared in trails towards the door, like some bodies had already been removed. My guess was that the police had fought their way in, multiple casualties on both sides (judging by the copious amount of yellow goo alongside the blood), and then dragged the bodies out of the lobby. I spotted a discarded firearm, and picked it up. I had no idea if it was loaded, or even how to check, but I tucked it into my pants anyway.

There was no one at reception. A sign, scrawled in biro and dotted with blood, said, *Back in 5*. Something electrical sparked overhead. Leaning on the baseball bat, I looked at the map, figuring Cassie would be in the ICU, unless she had made a run for it. I had to assume she was still in the hospital, and needed to let her know I was here.

The PA system would do the trick.

I climbed over the desk, landing on my feet on the other side. The body of a nurse lay prone, her blouse torn open. One of her breasts was a mangled, shredded mess, her face frozen in terror. I swallowed the sickness that rose in my throat, and picked up the PA mic, pressing the button.

"Cassie...it's Dan." My voice boomed out over the speakers. "I've come to get you. I'm gonna head to ICU." A noise somewhere, a door opening. I paused, then pressed the button on the mic again. "Hope you're there, baby."

I had to assume that the creatures didn't understand English. If they did, I could expect to find quite the welcoming party when I arrived. According to the map, the ICU was on the second floor, far end of the building.

Great.

I nervously tapped at the gun, just to check it was still there, then lifted the bat, waiting for a non-existent pitcher.

The battle raged outside, gunfire exchanged, people screaming.

There was no turning back now.

## 12

THE FIRST FLOOR WAS TOO QUIET.

The cafe was open, or had been, the smell of coffee mingling with the stink of death. I peered over the side at a dozen mangled bodies scattered across the floor, covered in those familiar bite marks. What did the creatures want? To eat us, or just kill us?

A TV played in the corner of the cafe. The president was onscreen, taking questions from the press, flanked by security. None of them were wearing a mask.

"Well what we have here is a, uh, situation involving an unknown orgasm...organim...organism. I'm told it's all in hand, and that—"

I couldn't listen to anymore of his lies, his bullshit. I stalked down the endless corridor. There were signs up everywhere, most hand-written, warning about the virus, and PPE, and face masks, and social distancing.

The works.

None of it would do any good any more. We were past the point of containment, or delaying the virus. Now, it was all down to survival. Could I do it? I had done pretty well so far, I supposed, though I was beginning to realize how tired I was. I hadn't eaten since yesterday, and even then, the small pot of microwave noodles hadn't exactly satisfied. I passed a vending machine, and smashed it with the bat, grabbing a candy bar and wolfing it down. Energy. That was what I needed. A sugar hit. I ate another, then carried on, coming to the elevators. Did I risk it? The stairs might be safer. No, I figured they wouldn't be smart enough to know how elevators work. I pressed the button and waited.

It was on level four, the top floor. The lights changed as it descended, counting down. It made me uneasy.

Three.

Two.

One.

I stepped back, gripping the old wooden bat, and the doors *whooshed* open. The creature came flying at me, coated in blood, claws extended. I reacted quickly, more out of fear than anything else, and caught it on the side of the head. It crashed to the ground, and I followed, bringing the bat down on its skull, pulping it.

I hadn't seen the second one.

It struck me in the back, winding me, and I fell forwards as it dragged its talons down my spine. I hit the ground, smacking my chin, letting go of the bat. It rolled away in a semi-circle, and I whirled onto my back, the creature scuttling up my legs, jaws snapping. I covered my face, and it bit down on my left arm, the teeth sinking into my flesh. Burning agony seared up my arm, as it closed its mouth, ripping out a chunk of muscle. It chewed greedily, and I could see my own tissue inside its slobbering mouth, a strip dangling down the small, spiky chin. I roared in pain, for what else could I do? The bat was out of reach, and—

Fuck!

Still defending myself with my savaged left arm, I reached down to my pants, searching for the gun. It was tucked into my waistband, and my fingers found it, the creature snapping its slobbering jaws inches from my face.

I grabbed the gun, unleashed it, and held it to the creature's neck as it swallowed.

I paused a second, feeling like the coolest motherfucker who ever lived, and said, "Here's your fucking vaccine." I smiled and pulled the trigger.

The gun was empty.

"Oh fuck fuck fuck!"

The mutation's jaws opened wide like a snake ready to devour its prey. Blood sprayed from my mauled arm, pouring over me. I raised my other arm, crossing them in front of me, and closed my eyes.

There was a wild thudding sound, and warm liquid gushed over my face. It stank of medical waste and pus, but there was no pain. I waited for something to happen. Was I dead?

Cautiously, I opened my eyes. The creature wobbled precariously a moment, then toppled to the side. Its head was missing. In my periphery, I could see a figure standing, dressed in white.

An angel.

Wait, an angel with a baseball bat?

"You came for me," the angel said, and my heart skipped.

"Cassie?"

She let go of the bat and knelt by me, helping me sit up. We embraced, and it had never felt better. Well, top three, alongside the first time we had made love, and after we said our vows. At least those times I wasn't hemorrhaging blood and stinking of municipal waste.

"I can't believe it," she said through tears that wet my cheek, her breath warm and beautiful and perfect.

"I said I'd be here," I grunted, trying to smile, wincing in pain. Reluctantly, we parted. She was wearing a hospital gown, spattered yellow with the blood of those creatures. I wondered how many she had already killed. She was a keeper, alright. A real keeper.

"You're bleeding," she said, looking at my arm.

"It bit me."

"Wait here." She got up and walked to the open elevator. The doors were trying to close, but a human arm was caught between them. She hit the button, and they opened fully. Her gown was open at the back, and I could see her bare ass. Unbelievably, I felt my dick stir, and laughed at the absurdity. There's just no telling that little guy, y'know?

She came out of the elevator holding a black leather belt.

"Where'd you get that from?" I asked. "Is that from a dead man?"

"You got a problem with that?"

I guess I didn't. Cassie wrapped it round my forearm, tightening it to stem the blood flow.

"Dan," she said. "Have you got an erection?"

"Well, uh…yeah." I looked up at her, tried to shrug. "I never thought I'd see your ass again."

"My…? Oh, Dan, for fuck's sake," she said, but she smiled lightly as she fastened the buckle on the belt. "My sister always said she wanted to find a man who looked at her the way that you look at my butt."

I would have been happy to talk about her ass all day, but time was running out. Outside the battle raged. There was a tremendous explosion, and it sounded like the militia had brought one of the helicopters down.

"What's happening, Cass? What the fuck is going on?"

Her smile faded. "I don't know. It started yesterday. These things," she said, gesturing at the creatures, "they live inside the virus. They feed on your insides, and then…Dan, we have to get out of here."

"I know."

"I fought my way down from ICU, but the cops wouldn't let us leave. They barricaded the doors. I've been sheltering in a supply closet for hours. When I heard you over the PA, I almost thought I was dreaming. How did you get in?"

"There's a riot outside. I snuck in during the chaos."

"Yeah, figures. Sounds like World War III out there."

"I wouldn't be surprised."

She wiped the yellow goop from my face. "Think we can get out that way?"

I shook my head. "That's the problem. The riot? I…I kinda started it."

She gave me a look that was half eye-roll, half love. "You what? I leave you alone for one week, and you start a new Civil War?"

"It's a long story. Maybe I'll tell you some day. But for now, if we go out there, we're gonna have two hundred gun-toting fuck-sticks after us."

"Upstairs is crawling with those things."

"How'd you get past them?"

She looked away from me. "I killed them, Dan. I killed as many as I could." Her eyes filled with tears. "I was going to be discharged today. I felt okay. My lungs are fucked, and I can't run, but other than that…I'm not too bad. The others up there though…they didn't stand a chance."

"You did what you had to do."

"I didn't save anyone. I was just thinking about myself… and you."

Glass shattered down the corridor, guns firing, people shouting, chanting.

*"USA, USA, USA."*

"I think your friends have arrived," said Cassie.

"Then let's get the fuck outta here."

*"There he is!"*

Shit. Cassie helped me stand, and together — at last, *together* — we ran to the elevator. She pulled the dead doctor's arm out the way of the doors, and a bullet clanged off the inside of the elevator. Cassie slammed the buttons, the doors closing. I could hear the footsteps of the militia, drawing closer, closer…the elevator started, and we pulled away from them, the gunshots muffled, getting quieter as we rose.

The carnage in the cramped space was horrendous. Doctors and nurses, one wearing a plastic visor, the others with cloth tied over their faces, lay shredded, their skin hanging in tattered ribbons.

"Where are we going?" I asked.

"I don't know. Those things are everywhere. What about the roof?"

"I've not had much luck with rooftops today," I said, thinking of Apple.

"You got a better suggestion?"

There was a colossal bang as something landed on top of the elevator. The carriage shook, and then stopped.

"What was that?" I said, though we both knew the answer.

"It's on the roof," said Cassie.

"Why have we stopped?"

"It's probably designed to stop when there's an impact." She jabbed the buttons again, but nothing happened. Something scratched noisily above us. We looked at each other uneasily. The light pat of curious footsteps circled above us.

We were stuck, trapped, unable to do anything but wait and listen to the thing above us scratch and paw at the ceiling.

It was trying to find a way in.

Four claws punctured the thin metal escape hatch, and we threw ourselves back against the walls.

"Shit, that won't last long!" I said. "Help me get the doors open."

I tried to slip my fingers between them, my left arm useless. Cassie joined me, as the scrabbling claws above us made short work of the hatch.

"Hurry!" said Cassie. Together, we forced the doors apart. We were between floors, with about twelve inches of the lower level visible at our feet. It wasn't a lot, but it had to be enough.

"Go through," I urged, and Cassie hit the floor, shimmying foot-first through the gap. A gray arm burst through the hatch, slashing recklessly, the claws inches from my face. I backed into the corner. Cassie was almost through, hanging over the edge. She let go, landing on her feet. "You okay?" I said.

"I'm fine," she answered quickly. "Hand me the bat, I can see one of those things."

I ducked down, and passed it through to her, just as the hatch gave way and the creature tumbled into the elevator with me. It landed with a bang, and the elevator started to move. The creature dived towards me, and I threw myself to the side, its head denting the metal panel.

"Cassie!" I shouted, but I could see her in the corridor, swinging the bat, striking another creature across the body. The elevator continued its descent, the full doorway opening. I tried to get past the creature, but it blocked my way. I needed a weapon. It came for me, and I grabbed one of the doctors' bodies, holding it as a human shield. The creature bit into the corpse's face, the sound of teeth grinding on bone making me nauseous. I shoved the body to one side, the creature still attached to it, and leaped through the narrowing gap. It came after me as I rolled into the corridor, reaching one arm through, but then the elevator was gone, slicing the creature's foul limb off. The severed appendage twitched and shook, yellow slime bubbling from the stump.

I looked up, and Cassie was there. One creature lay dead at her feet. Another prowled the corridor in front of her. She stood ready, legs apart, holding the bat, gown flowing open, ass showing once again. "Come and get me, motherfucker," she spat.

I had never, in all my life, felt more in love.

Suddenly I heard more footsteps. Lots of them, coming from the other end of the corridor. The militia. Jesus, could they please and kindly *fuck the fuck off?* I hadn't touched old Pops, that piece of shit. He had killed *my* friend. I looked back and saw the creature running for Cassie. She got ready to swing, and at the last second, I grabbed her and pulled her out of the way, dragging her into one of the wards. The creature didn't stop. Its footsteps echoed through the corridor, until ferocious gunfire tore through the hospital.

I closed the door, but there was no lock.

The ward was a grisly nightmare. Slain bodies lay in beds, on the floor, some of them in pieces, torn limb-from-bloody-limb.

"What floor did we make it to?" I asked.

"I think we're on three."

"So we still have one to go. Shit."

"We can make it," said Cassie. Her voice, as always,

soothed me, but there was no time for sentimentality. As I leaned against the wall to catch my breath, the door burst open. A member of the militia strode purposefully in, the door hiding me. He raised a shotgun, pointed it at Cassie.

"Hey, you seen a man in here?" he grunted. He wore the requisite militia uniform of camouflage shorts, a black tee with a howling wolf on the back, black sunglasses, and that stupid fucking cap.

"What man?" said Cassie. She never once glanced at me, nor gave my location away. The door swung shut.

"Young guy, glasses. He killed Pops, and we're gonna kill him. This is the start of the, uh, new world order." He sounded like he was reciting from memory. I shuffled to the side, nearing a small fire extinguisher.

"Everyone's dead," Cassie said, convincingly shell-shocked. "I think I'm the only one left."

He never had a chance to respond. I brought the extinguisher down on his head, the red MAGA cap an ideal bullseye. There was a violent crunch, and the man sagged to the floor. I picked up the shotgun.

"You know how to use that?" said Cassie.

"No. You?"

"No."

"Then I'll figure it out. Where are the stairs?"

She thought a moment. "Left, then left again."

"You sure?"

"Of course not. I've been on a ventilator all week."

I nodded. "Point taken." I peered out through a crack in the door. No trace of the militia, or the creatures. Cassie had said there were hundreds...so where were they? Had they congregated on level two? And if so, had we bypassed them all in the elevator?

Or — and let's face it, this was the more likely scenario — were they all on level four? I pushed the thought aside.

"Let's go," I said, creeping out into the corridor. It was quiet. Far, far too quiet. Cassie stuck close to me. I could feel her pressing against my back, hear her shallow breathing. I paused, and turned to her.

"I love you," I said.

She smiled. "Why'd you say that?"

"Because for a while there…I thought I'd never be able to tell you again. When the medics took you away…I thought it was the last time."

"I never thought that," she said, and touched my uninjured arm.

"So how about it? You want to say anything back?"

She leaned forward and kissed me. "Maybe later," she said. "And there *will be* a later."

I wished I had her confidence. I started down the corridor, sweeping the gun in front of me like I'd seen people do in the movies.

Gunfire, somewhere ahead of us.

Or behind.

It was hard to tell, the way the corridors twisted and turned back on themselves.

A militia member staggered backwards out of a doorway, something clinging to his face. I raised the gun and fired, got lucky. The creature hit the wall, taking the man's face with it. He crashed to his knees, eyeballs darting back and forth across a dark red skull. I held the gun to his head, ready to put him out of his misery.

"No," said Cassie. I looked at her. "Conserve your ammo."

She raised the bat and smashed his skull. I pointed at the pistol in his hand. "You want it?"

"I'm fine with this," she said, nodding at the bat.

"Never took you as a baseball fan."

"Never took you as a gun nut."

We turned the second corner. A nurse lay in the middle of the corridor, her stomach wide open. We stepped over her. It's amazing how quickly you get used dead bodies. Was this the *new normal* the politicians over in the UK kept talking about?

"Something's coming," said Cassie.

I turned back, facing the way we'd come. I heard it too, multiple footsteps, too heavy to be the creatures.

"It could be the cops," I said.

"I don't think so."

They were closing in. One man dressed in that stupid-ass V For Vendetta mask came skidding round the corner. He saw us and raised his gun, squeezing off a shot before I blasted him with the shotgun. His chest exploded, his bullet slamming into the wall right next to my head.

"Too close," I said. We ran.

*"He got Cyrus!"* shouted someone.

*"Fuckin' kill that bastard!"*

"Where are the stairs?" I shouted to Cassie.

"I told you, I wasn't sure!"

Doors, doors, an infinite amount of doors, but no stairs, no elevators, no *nothing*. Shots were fired, glass broke, brick shattered. Bullets whizzed by our ears, and then Cassie fell. She didn't scream as the bullet hit her. It was more of a surprised *ugh*. She slumped to the floor, blood seeping from the wound in her leg, a perfect round little bullet-hole just above her knee. I went to her, and we locked eyes, her steely look of determination spurring me on. Someone came careening round the corner. I raised my weapon and fired, but he was too fast, and I missed. He held a machete — a fucking *machete* — and came at us. Cassie, still on the floor, hurled her bat at him. It was some next-level Jackie Chan-type shit, and it smacked the bastard in his ankles. He hit the ground, and I hauled Cassie to her feet. She slung her arm over my shoulder, and we ran, the world's most desperate three-legged race.

"You okay?" I managed to ask.

"No," she said angrily. "He fucking *shot* me."

I saw double-doors ahead of us, and if my heart could have beat any faster, it would've.

"The stairs!"

"Give me the gun and carry me," said Cassie. Without waiting, she grabbed the shotgun from me, and jumped in front of me on her good leg. I lifted her in a one-armed bear-hug, Cassie facing the other way. She fired a shot, and something wet burst behind me.

"Got him," she said. "There're more. Hurry, Dan!"

"Trying." She wasn't heavy, but my shoulders were in bad shape, and my left arm was pretty much out of use. I was running on adrenaline.

She fired again, and then several bullets hit the wall nearby.

"These assholes aim like stormtroopers," cried Cassie with glee, like she was really enjoying this. I had to admit, it made a change from being stuck in the apartment all day, drinking myself into an early grave.

"Brace yourself," I said, as we hit the doors.

We entered the stairwell. A sign pointed up to level four. There had to be away onto the roof from there. And then what? Signal for a copter? They'd probably shoot us where we stood. But, I've said it before, and I'll say it again.

*Fuck it.*

I trudged up the stairs, Cassie seeming to grow heavier

with each step. She slipped, and I adjusted my hand under her ass cheek, supporting her as best I could.

"Watch those fingers," she said.

"It's not deliberate."

"Sure, sure." She fired again, the blast reverberating throughout the stairs, still echoing as we made it to the final set of doors. I kicked them open, wondering how many bullets we had left, and walked inside, unprepared for what we would find in there.

# PART III

The Golden Tears of Venom

## 13

"What the fuck," I said. There were no other words.

The fourth level — which, according to the sign, should have housed the orthopedic and gynecology wards — had been transformed.

Into what, I wasn't sure.

Cassie held my waist, favoring her undamaged leg. We clung to each other in shock.

The corridor looked like it was made of human flesh, the walls sinewy and pink. You ever see footage from inside the human body, when the doctor shoves a microscopic camera down some poor sap's throat? It was like that, but moist and humid. The ceiling dripped thick globs of slime, the ground sticky, sucking at our feet.

The walls seemed to pulsate...to *breathe*.

I heard the footsteps coming up the stairs, but I couldn't take my eyes off the sinister, pulsing light at the end of the corridor. It glowed pink, then red, then yellow, a neon spectrum of ineffable madness.

Its glow drew me in, and I had to fight to resist. Cassie took a step towards it.

"It's beautiful," she said.

I nodded. "It's dangerous."

"We've got no choice."

She was right, as usual. She always was. It was just another reason why I loved her. We headed off down the corridor. Otherworldly fauna blossomed spectacularly along the floor, the walls, the ceiling, puckering and spitting, weeping ghastly golden tears of venom. The doors behind us opened, but when I turned, I could see nothing but the glow. It consumed everything, a black hole of wild color, if that made any sense.

*"What is this queer shit?"* said one of militia, I guess because in his pea-brain, colors are gay or something.

"Come on," I said, helping Cassie limp away from them. We ducked into a room, the door covered with stringy pink mucus that broke like silken spiderwebs at my touch. Inside, I saw a large window, and we walked solemnly towards it. It didn't face out onto the street. Rather, it overlooked what had once been an operating theater. We pressed our palms to the glass, staring in stunned awe.

It was an egg.

It must have been fifteen foot tall, pink and magnificent in all its sepulchral splendor, a throbbing, bulbous ovum covered in lumps and sores. The creatures lined up before it, patiently waiting. The one at the front of the queue moved closer, pressing a paw to the fleshy sac, and the egg absorbed it, the creature howling as it was pulled inside, breaking apart, the limbs torn asunder until no trace of its existence remained.

Then the next creature stepped forward.

"What's happening?" I said.

"This is how it ends," said Cassie. "For all of us."

The egg grew in size with each absorption. It glowed,

*The Blood Beast Mutations*

faintly at first, quickly finding its full bloom. Something moved inside, long, skeletal...huge. It pressed against the walls of the egg, which bulged outwards. One-by-one, the creatures continued their thoughtless sacrifice.

Someone walked into the room with us.

"We got you now," said a man's voice.

"I don't wanna shoot you in the back," said another. "Turn the fuck around."

But I couldn't tear my eyes away. I felt Cassie take my hand, our fingers entwining. The egg cracked, the walls drooping and flopping to the side, bilious liquid flooding the operating room.

Something was emerging.

"This isn't a good time," I said to the assembled throng.

"Now is definitely the time, you fuck. Now drop your weapon, and turn and face me like a man, or so help me God, I will blow your fucking brains out."

"Hey, his chick has a nice ass. Wouldn't mind a ride on that." That was Junior. He was a lot braver now he was backed up by a small army.

Spindly tentacles erupted from the egg, shooting around the operating theater. The remaining creatures fled. One grasping limb grazed the window, cracked it.

"What was that?" asked Junior. "What's in there?"

Cassie looked at me. We both knew time was up.

"Let's find out," I said. With my back to the men, I raised my gun, took aim at the egg, and fired.

## 14

The glass broke, and as it did, Cassie and I hit the deck, turning to face the militia. At least ten of them were crammed into the room, who knows how many more out there. A couple of them had their guns trained on us, but most were transfixed by the insane golden glow from the operating theater, like the morning sun was rising in there. They covered their eyes, shielding them from the hellish light, aiming their guns at it. I supposed shooting at a light was no more stupid than shooting at a virus.

Turns out nature doesn't give a shit about your second amendment.

What happened next was a blur. The leader of the militia — a gray-haired dude in a bandana, khaki shorts, and a bandolier — stiffened, blood spraying out the back of his head. I thought at first he'd been shot, until I saw the semi-transparent tentacle jutting out between his eyes. Blood spurted along the inside of the tentacle, small chunks of gray brain matter too. The man vibrated, as his insides were sucked through the tentacle like a plastic straw. The men panicked and started firing. At least three of them dropped dead, victims of friendly fire, the bullets ricocheting around the room. I dragged Cassie into the corner, as two enormous purple hands settled on the frame of the window, and then dozens more tentacles fired out. They struck the militia members in the front row, easily penetrating their body armor. Their skin shriveled like raisins, mouths turning to tiny black circles set in hollow gray faces, eyes rolling upwards.

Then the face of the monster appeared.

I looked away, but not before glimpsing the bloated, tumefied head, covered in what looked like thousands of beady, black eyes.

More men opened fire, the shots lighting up the room with the blaze of gunfire, but nothing fazed the abomination as it clambered effortlessly through the window. It swung a taloned hand out towards the men, slicing Junior across his belly. He stood a moment, wobbling the way that Apple had when they had shot her, before his guts spilled out onto the floor and lay there steaming.

Terrified, the men scattered. A tentacle wrapped round one of their necks, squeezing so hard that it sliced through his neck in seconds, the head popping off and rolling across the floor, trampled under the feet of the retreating militia. The beast emerged fully, glowing energy pulsing through its limbs, and stood, smashing into the ceiling. The roof cracked, masonry crumbling in miniature waterfalls.

I looked up. The ceiling was caving in.

The monster grabbed another man from the stampede, holding him by the head and feet, pulling him in two, his body tearing like a wet tissue, the floor awash in blood. It tried to follow them through the door, but the roof could take no more. It crashed down around us, huge concrete blocks smashing through the floor.

Part of the ceiling drooped, forming a semi pathway to the roof.

"Cassie!" I shouted. "Come on!"

She nodded in understanding.

The neon beast was trying to force its massive bulk through the doorway. Over the sound of gunfire and screaming, I could hear the spinning rotor blades of a helicopter.

Daylight poured in through the ceiling, as Cassie clung on to my shoulder. We ran for the incline, scrambling onto the roof, the stonework cracking beneath our feet.

A fire broke out below, sprinklers going off, alarms sounding, as we made it onto the roof, running as far from the collapsing area as possible, heading for the edge of the building. We reached it, looking out over the carnage.

The creatures swarmed the streets, feasting on the flesh of the dead. Some people ran screaming, the creatures picking them off, knocking them down, tearing them apart. The skyline was black with smoke from multiple fires raging all across the city.

A few members of the militia remained, blockaded by vehicles, impotently shooting their guns at the mass of writhing mutants. They would run out of ammo eventually, and when they did…

A copter circled overhead. There was one pilot, one sniper, and plenty of space for passengers.

"Hey!" I screamed, waving my hand. "Down here!"

Cassie joined in. "Help us! Please"

The pilot seemed to notice. The copter swooped down from the skies, hovering above the roof, trying to find a safe place to land. Unable to do so, he motioned us towards him, and we stumbled groggily towards the rescue vehicle.

I saw the cracks hastening their way across the roof, and

before I had a chance to say anything, Cassie screamed. When I turned, she was gone. I lay down, spreading my weight, and saw her hands clutching desperately against the roof. She slid, fingernails scraping across the rough stone, three of them snapping clean off.

"Cassie," I shouted, crawling towards her, grabbing her hand. I looked down into the gap, gripping onto Cassie's wrist, as she dangled over the edge. Level four had collapsed, and she was a good forty-feet above the next level. Fires raged beneath, huge sparks blasting uncontrollably from ruined electrical equipment.

Deep, resonant thuds pounded through the building.

"Dan, it's coming! I can see it! *Oh god help me!*"

She was slipping through my grasp, my hand sweaty, weak. I looked over to the copter, the pilot watching me, unable to land, but waiting, just in case.

"I got you," I said, the strain etched onto my face. I tried to pull her up, but my arm felt like it would tear free. Blood poured from the rapidly widening wounds in my shoulder, my other arm numb and useless and blue, the belt tightly wound around it.

Cassie looked up at me, eyes rimmed with tears. I could tell what she was thinking. She didn't have to say a word.

"No fucking way," I said through gritted teeth. "It's both of us, or neither of us."

I swung my other arm over the gap, the footsteps of the giant mutation causing the building to shudder like an earthquake.

"Grab on to the belt," I said.

"I can't reach!"

I tried to swing her, one way, and then the other, giving her the momentum to reach up and grab me. Her bleeding fingertips brushed the leather belt, but didn't catch.

The pilot waited. I could hear the copter, feel the air rushing across the rooftop.

"Dan, it's almost here!" cried Cassie. With all my strength, I swung her away, and then towards me again. This time she caught the belt. I bent my arm at the elbow to stop it from sliding off, and tried to stand. I adjusted my position so that my feet were on the ground in a crouch, and put my back into it. It wasn't enough. I had nothing left.

The tank was empty.

The agony that coursed through my body rendered me speechless, tears falling down my cheeks.

I lost my footing and fell, sliding towards the gap.

It was over. All over.

Two burly hands closed over my shoulders, stopping me. I looked into the face of the sniper, most of it hidden by dark glasses and the biggest ear-protectors I'd ever seen.

"I got you," he said in a thick, European-sounding accent.

"Cassie," I said, and he understood. He leaned into the gap, lifting Cassie out, making it look easy. I guess if you can keep a sniper rifle steady in a helicopter, you've probably got mean upper body strength. He laid her next to me, then turned to us.

"We've got to—"

His body jerked, mouth opening soundlessly.

A lungful of blood splattered the ground. Tentacles — more than I could count — thrust out of the gap, stabbing into him. They pierced his arms, his legs, his back, his head, whipping wildly, jostling for prime position.

The cracks widened around us. I took a last look at our rescuer, that hero, and knew it was too late. The tentacles were sucking him dry, leaving a skeleton draped in loose gray fabric.

*The Blood Beast Mutations*

I looked at Cassie.

"Get to the chopper!" I shouted, and I swear to god she laughed at me. I couldn't understand why. Scrambling to our feet, we ran for the copter. I say 'ran', but by now, we were — to use a medical term — totally fucked.

The pilot signaled, screaming something. The ground underfoot seemed to slope, until it felt like we were running uphill, the copter never seeming to get any closer.

Something roared behind us. The monster.

The queen.

The chopper was ten feet away, but we were moving so slowly, goddammit!

"Hurry!" I think the pilot screamed, though I couldn't hear him.

We reached the vehicle, hovering just above the rapidly collapsing roof, and I helped Cassie in first. I followed, climbing in and rolling onto the floor, next to my wife, my incredible wife.

The helicopter lifted, not waiting for us to strap ourselves in. From our vantage point, we could see the devastation of the hospital. The roof had almost entirely disintegrated. Huge flames flared up from below, surrounding the neon creature. It had doubled in size, now standing about thirty, thirty-five foot high.

Cassie clung to me. Neither of us spoke.

The city we loved, and had lived in all our lives, had been totaled. It was a ruin, a wasteland. How many of those monsters were there? How many more were rampaging across the city, the country...the world?

Was this it? Was this the end of everything, of the world we knew, of life itself?

As we pulled away from the hospital, I watched the creature, feeling irrationally jealous.

It was their world now.

We had a good run, but now it was *game over, no lives left, hope you had a great time, please do not put another coin into the slot.*

The creature watched us curiously, reaching up one long, slimy arm. For a crazy moment, I thought it was waving goodbye. The air seemed to move in front of it, and I realized what I was looking at.

The transparent tentacles.

"Move!" I shouted at the pilot, but the roar of the rotor blades was too loud.

I grabbed Cassie and flattened us, the air fizzing just overhead as the appendages shot by. The pilot was not so lucky. One embedded itself in his arm, the copter tilting as he lost control. I got to my feet, clinging on for dear life, and climbed between the cockpit seats. Gripping the tentacle with both hands, I tried to rip it, tear it, to no avail. I was almost out of options.

But there was one thing left to try.

As the pilot's blood seeped along the ghastly limb, I opened my mouth wide, bared my teeth, and bit down hard. The taste was revolting, horrifying, like slimy, raw chicken with the aftertaste of another man's blood. My teeth closed, snapping together, grinding through the rubbery mass, until the tentacle split in two.

The pilot yanked the dead flap of skin from his arm and hurled it from the sky. He took the controls, working the sticks, and then we were off, the hospital slipping from memory like a bad dream.

## 15

It's been ten days, and I still wake up screaming.

I expect I always will, but you never know. The human mind is surprisingly resilient.

Cassie wakes like that too, but she usually manages to fall back asleep, and in the morning, forgets she even had the nightmare again.

We're on an island now.

I don't know where, and I don't care. It's hot, there's sand between my toes, and my girl is by my side.

She's next to me right now, fast asleep, naked beneath the thin cotton sheet. She stirs as I run my hand over the gentle curves of her body, and I let her rest a little longer. The sun is up, and it's gonna be another glorious day.

Getting here was hell. We stopped countless times to refuel, Cassie taking the sniper rifle, picking off the few creatures that remained. Most of the smaller ones are gone now, and sightings of the queens have dropped, or so I read on the internet.

It's funny. I always thought that only cockroaches would

survive an apocalypse. Turns out, it's cockroaches and BuzzFeed.

The creatures are disappearing. According to official reports, the army have brought a few of the bigger ones down safely, though there's a Facebook Live video out there showing what looks to be a nuclear explosion in the middle of Detroit, before the person filming it is obliterated by the seismic blast.

I try not to think of what we saw on our journey here, that gigantic, pulsating egg in the stadium, six or seven of the monster queens queuing up in front of it.

I try *never* to think of that.

Cassie turns over, putting her arms around me, her breasts pressing into my side. She kisses my neck, rolls on top of me, and tells me she loves me. I tell her I love her too.

I don't know if things will ever go back to the way they were, but we're taking one day at a time. There's talk of attempting to get to New Zealand. Apparently, they wiped the virus out before the mutations began.

But that can wait. For now, we're all just trying to heal.

America is gone. Finished. All the guns in the fucking world, and they couldn't stop anything.

Cassie kisses my lips and rolls off me. She picks up her phone.

"The president's giving his address. Wanna watch?" she says.

I sigh. "Go on then, let's see what he has to say."

The connection is slow, but it still works. The video comes on, and there he is, holed up in a dimly-lit room. He sits there, cloaked in shadow.

"I'm coming to you live, from, uh, the presidential bunker." He sounds tired. "As many of you know, thousands of lives have been lost due to the deadly Chinese Virus—"

"Thousands?" says Cassie. She laughs. "There's barely a thousand people left."

The president continues.

"—to prevent any further damage to the economy, workplaces must reopen on Monday. Too many God-fearing, hard-working Americans are being—"

"Does he not know no one's left?" I say.

Cassie leans her head against my shoulder. "The money's gone now. All he has left to care about are the ratings."

"—The LameStream media haven't reached out to me, but..." He trails off for a moment. "What's that noise?"

He shuffles his notes, backs away from the desk.

"I don't know, Mr. President," says someone offscreen.

"I thought this place was sealed up tight?"

"It was, but we had to send a recon team out to look for a McDonald's, remember?"

I look at Cassie. She's smiling. She can hear it too.

"What the fuck *is* that?" says the president.

"It sounds like insects."

"Well get them out of here." He shrieks. "Something bit me!"

"Oh my god, there's too many!"

The president stands up, walks backwards into the light. He's pale white, his head as bald as an eagle. He's not wearing any pants. The image is suddenly overcome by a whirring mass of enormous insects. The president screams.

"Oh shit...it's the murder hornets!"

They obscure the screen, and we listen for a while to the wretched, dying screams of the president and his VP. It's the only sincere emotion I've ever heard him utter. The feed doesn't end.

For all we know, it'll go on forever.

Cassie switches the phone off, places it face down. She gets up and walks naked onto the beach, the waves lapping against the shore. She turns and beckons me, and I get out of bed and follow her into the water, the sun on my face.

Life goes on.

## AFTERWORD

You may find the very idea of this book tasteless, and you may be right. But just know, it came from a place of anger.

We need to look out for each other.

Stay safe, my friends.

Printed in Great Britain
by Amazon